DON'T PROMISE ME RAINBOWS

DON'T PROMISE ME RAINBOWS

•

SUSAN AYLWORTH

AVALON BOOKS
THOMAS BOUREGY AND COMPANY, INC.
401 LAFAYETTE STREET
NEW YORK, NEW YORK 10003

PRINTED IN THE UNITED STATES OF AMERICA
ON ACID-FREE PAPER
BY HADDON CRAFTSMEN, SCRANTON, PENNSYLVANIA

For my dear ones:
For Aaron and Barbara,
For Adam, Jared, and Matt,
For John, who felt left out of the last book,
For Paul and Rebecca,
And always, for Roger.

Chapter One

No doubt about it, Jezebel was in trouble. She lay on her side in the farrowing pen, groaning and making hard little grunting noises, her pink trotters thrashing the new straw. She'd been like this for more than an hour. Chris groaned too, combing fingers through his shoulder-length blond hair in abject frustration.

A sharp noise from down the aisle sent him scurrying to check on Flossie. He grimaced as he looked at her. Flossie wasn't doing any better than Jezebel. Chris drew in a deep breath and blew it out through his teeth. It was nothing but foul luck that put two of his best sows into labor at the same time, both with difficult births.

He had checked Jezebel a few minutes ago. Experience told him the first piglet was large and turned sideways, blocking the space so the rest of the litter couldn't be delivered, and positioned so it was impossible for Chris to get a hold of it. Then while Chris was working with Jezebel, Flossie had started groaning. He'd checked her too, and found exactly the same problem. One difficult birth he could probably handle, but two?

He straightened. What he needed was help. From habit, he thought first of his brothers, but Jim was on a business trip in California and had taken his wife and baby daughter with him. Kurt was honeymooning with his new bride; they wouldn't return for another week. Luck again. Here he was, in need of help and fresh out of brothers.

Even his mother, who lived on the farm, was away this week, visiting his sister Joan and his brother-in-law Bob, helping their three little children through a bout of chicken pox. Chris was on his own, smack-dab in the middle of Rainbow Rock, Arizona.

A sharp squeal brought him out of his reverie. Flossie was clearly in pain. The litter needed to be delivered, and fast. Dashing to the end of the hallway, he yanked the telephone off the hook and punched in the number for Doc Richards's office. The family vet for more than thirty years, the doc had seen more birthing emergencies in more varieties of large animals than most people ever heard of. He'd even delivered a camel once. If there was anyone qualified to help in this emergency, it was Richards. The phone rang three times before a female voice answered, "Richards Veterinary."

Caught off guard, Chris stammered, "I-I want to speak to Richards."

"He isn't in today. How may I help you?"

"Where can I find him?"

"What's your emergency?"

Chris felt his knuckles whitening on the receiver. "Look, I need to talk to Doc Richards. Can you put me in touch with him? *Now?*"

The woman sighed. What did *she* have to be impatient about? He made a mental note to talk with Richards about his pushy new receptionist. "Dr. Richards is unavailable. What's your emergency?"

Chris bit his lip, becoming angrier by the moment; but he was beginning to realize that if he wanted any help at all, he was going to have to play this woman's game. He could tell her she was an officious Amazon later, after Flossie and Jezebel were okay. Steadying himself, he said, "This is Chris McAllister at Rainbow Rock Farms. I have two sows farrowing, both in trouble. Both seem to have first piglets presenting in unusual ways. Neither can deliver without help and I'm alone here."

"How long are the labors?" It sounded like the woman was taking notes.

"The first has been trying to deliver for about twenty minutes; the second, maybe fifteen. I called as soon as I could. Look, I need the doctor. Can you find him for m—"

"I'll be right there." The line went dead.

"I'll"? Had the officious Amazon said *"I'll"?* Chris put the phone down and hurried back to Flossie.

She was still struggling to deliver, her whole body pulsing with each contraction. Feeling helpless, Chris went back to Jezebel, who was now straining harder than ever. He needed Doc Richards and he needed him now. Fearing he was on his own, Chris pulled on sterile gloves and decided to do what he could for Jez.

Several long minutes and one good kick from Jezebel later, Chris had managed to push the badly positioned piglet back far enough that he could get a finger on the creature's snout. After that it took only a few seconds of groping before he located the two front feet. With a quick tug, he jerked the trotters around into the birth canal. Jezebel heaved, thrusting away from him, and he lost his grip, but before he could try again, she was delivering. With the logjam broken, the little porker slid out into the straw, feet first as nature had intended. "Good for you, Jez!" Chris said encouragingly, then knelt to have a look at the little one.

He was a boar, as Chris had suspected, and a big one for certain, bigger than most newborns by far—maybe ten inches. But something was wrong. A quick check revealed that although the little guy had a heartbeat, he wasn't breathing. Chris quickly flipped him to his back and began massaging his abdomen, pressing the pads of two fingers into the little fellow's diaphragm. It took three tries, then there was a hissing sound—like air released from a bike tire—and the piglet took a breath. Exultant, Chris rocked back on his heels, just in time to see Jezebel deliver a second piglet, this one a tiny sow that squealed almost as soon as she hit the straw.

"Good work, Jezebel," he repeated, stroking the sow's side. She grunted in apparent satisfaction and delivered a third healthy baby. Deciding she was doing well enough on her own, Chris stood, determined to do what he could for Flossie, but a close examination had already told him that her case was more difficult than Jezebel's. He tensed his jaw. Then, as he started toward Flossie's stall, he heard a truck pull up outside.

He gave Flossie a quick check first. Nothing seemed changed. Then he strode toward the doorway and out into the sunlight. It was Doc Richards' truck. *Wiley C. Richards, D.V.M.* gleamed in sedate black lettering along the panels of the back. But the slim, fragile-looking redhead who slipped from behind the wheel certainly wasn't Doc Richards. She barely looked big enough to lift the medical kit she was wrestling off the front passenger seat. *This* was the officious Amazon?

Uncertain of how he should proceed, Chris asked, "Where's the doc?"

"*I'm* the doc," the redhead answered, not even looking up as she unloaded various tools from the back of the panel truck, putting them into her medical bag. "Sarah McGill, D.V.M., University of Arizona. I even have a license to practice, issued by the state last spring." She straightened, giving him a withering look. "Now, where's my patient?"

Chris hooked a thumb toward the farrowing shed. "In here." He turned, leading the way, wondering as he walked what this petite young woman could do with a sow more than twice her size. When he arrived at Flossie's stall, the redhead opened the gate and slipped past him, dropping to her knees at Flossie's side while Chris was still wondering how she got in there so quickly. She barely took a moment to examine the sow. "Do you have some heavy twine? Baling twine, maybe?"

Chris bristled at her take-charge attitude, but answered anyway. "Sure. There's a basket near the door where we keep the twine off the straw bales."

"Bring some. Quickly. Then get in here and help me if you can."

"Sure thing," Chris grumbled, and moved to comply. He still had serious doubts about whether this little slip of a thing could do anything when he couldn't, but if she stood a chance of saving Flossie and her litter, he had to give her a try. He was back promptly, carrying the twine.

"Good," the redhead said, barely looking up at him. She had put on sterile gloves and was now busy working near Flossie's belly, injecting something into the sow's haunch. "Unravel that twine, then come help me."

"Right," Chris growled, but under his breath he added, "You'd darn well better know what you're doing."

"Okay," the redhead said, looking up at him. "I'm going to try to get a loop around the little one, around a foot if I can. If not, I may have to put the loop around its neck. Once the loop is fixed, I'll need you to hold the sow on her side with two feet in the air while I use the twine to yank the piglet. We might lose this baby in the process, but we can save the sow and the rest of the litter. Are you ready?''

''Yeah,'' Chris answered, moving to Flossie's side.

For several long seconds, she fumbled with the pig and the twine, then looked up with a triumphant grin. ''Got it!'' she said. ''Roll her up. There. Okay, let's go,'' she instructed, giving the twine a firm, steady pull.

For several seconds, nothing seemed to happen, then miraculously, as if in slow motion, a snout emerged. Behind it came two front trotters, bent at the knees and turned back on themselves, then the rest of the piglet.

Chris watched, trying to remember to close his mouth. ''Amazing,'' he murmured when he regained his power of speech. The way those front trotters were turned backwards, he'd have sworn it would never work. But the lady vet wasn't through. ''Okay, he's free,'' she said, holding the little boar in both hands. ''Now let's see if we can get him started.'' She slipped the noose from around the piglet's neck and rolled him onto his back, rubbing life into him as Chris had done with the other stuck piglet minutes before.

Chris watched, admiring her skill and her care with the newborn pig. He noticed how red her hair was, almost coppery where it picked up stray shafts of sunlight. He noticed the snowdrop whiteness of her skin. He noticed too that her commands had softened as soon as the level of emergency diminished. She worked with an absolute economy of motion, palpating the piglet's diaphragm until he finally breathed. "That should do it," she said as she set him down. "How's Mama doing?"

"Just fine," Chris answered as he watched Flossie deliver her second piglet with ease.

"Great!" the redhead answered, relaxing for the first time since she'd arrived. She turned to Chris, blue-green eyes sparkling. "Now, where's the other one?"

"Other one?" Still impressed by what he'd just witnessed, Chris went blank.

"The other sow?" the woman prompted. "The unusual presentation?"

"Oh, Jezebel," he said. "I took care of her before you got here."

A look of confusion crossed her face, transforming itself into grudging respect. Something about her look, the turn of her head, reminded Chris of someone. "Mind if I look at her?" she asked.

"Of course not," Chris said. Suddenly feeling generous, he led the way down the aisle toward Jezebel's stall. They arrived just as Jez delivered another healthy piglet. The straw around her was littered with baby pigs.

"Looks like she's doing fine," the lady vet said approvingly. She rubbed Jezebel's ears and crooned, "Aren't you, sweetheart?" The pig snorted and leaned into the woman's hand. Chris stirred uneasily. He'd never felt envious of a pig before. The redhead gave

Jezebel a thorough once-over, then looked around. "You have standing racks?"

"Yeah," Chris answered.

"Okay if we get her into them? I think she's through delivering, and we wouldn't want her to roll over on one of these little guys by accident."

"Good idea," Chris answered. He walked to the sow's head. "Come on, Jez. Time to get up now." The pig, trained from years of human contact, obediently stood and followed him into the standing racks, where he rewarded her with an ample measure of grain. He fastened the gate behind her. All around the piglets swarmed in, each latching on to a teat.

"One, two . . ." the lady vet counted under her breath. "Looks like you've got sixteen healthy babies here."

Chris gloated. "Jez is one of our best producers. That's why I worry when she has a problem."

"I think everything is fine now," the redhead answered, her voice flat. There was an odd air of sadness about her. "Shall we check on Flossie again?" By the time they returned, Flossie had delivered eight and seemed well on her way to producing a record litter. "Everything looks fine here, too," the woman said as she began to pack up her things.

Chris remembered his business manners. "What do we owe you?"

"The office will send you a bill." She kept on packing.

Curious, Chris changed his tack. "So what happened to Doc Richards, anyway?" He leaned along the fence rail, watching her as she worked. He noticed the way her slim back moved beneath the fabric of her shirt and was surprised at the attraction he felt.

"Dad was kicked by a horse," she answered. "Broke his kneecap. I'm afraid he'll be out of commission for a few weeks yet." She spoke so matter-of-factly that the first word almost slipped by.

But Chris had heard it. "Dad?" he repeated slowly. "Doc Richards is your dad?" Then he knew why she looked familiar. "You're Sarah Richards!"

For a second, emotion flashed in her eyes, eyes almost as turquoise as the stones Navajo silversmiths worked into their jewelry. That heated look made Chris want to lick his lips, but it vanished almost as quickly as it had appeared. Sarah's voice was icy as she answered, "It's Sarah McGill—*Doctor* McGill to you, cowboy."

"Yes, ma'am," Chris answered, his face dimpling in a cheeky grin. "But you *were* Sarah Richards. I remember."

She looked perplexed. "You remember? But I don't remem—Wait a minute! You're the little brother, right? The one we used to call Goldilocks!"

Chris cringed. It had been at least ten years since anyone had called him Goldilocks. The last time, he'd been sixteen and finally starting to get some size. The kid who had used the hateful name had spent the next ten minutes getting his breath back and the following half-hour apologizing. "My name is Christopher Mc-Allister," he answered coolly. "That's Chris to you, Doc."

The lady grinned, her brilliant eyes twinkling. "That's a deal, Chris. And you can call me Sarah." She offered her hand.

Chris took her hand in his, holding it firmly. "Sarah," he answered, acknowledging her words. "Thank you for helping me with Flossie today."

She grinned. "That's what I'm here for." She dropped his hand and started to turn away.

He caught her arm, noticing as he did so that she wasn't wearing a wedding ring. What he wanted was to see those brilliant eyes flash again the way they had a few moments ago. "You know, Sarah McGill," he said, "for a nice-looking woman, you're not a bad animal doctor."

She lifted her chin, a defiant gesture, and her eyes flashed as he had hoped they would, but there was a look of pure mischief in them when she said, "I'd have said that for a brilliant veterinarian, I'm not bad looking." She pulled away from him, tossed him a look that almost curled his toes, hopped into her truck, then barreled down the gravel road, raising a plume of red dust in her wake.

"Wow," Chris whispered as he watched her go. He'd felt this way once before, when he was nine and an ornery mule had kicked him in the stomach, knocking the breath out of him. Only this time it felt good, really good. He wondered if, and when, he might see Sarah McGill again.

Late afternoon was one of Chris's favorite times. The farm lay quiet, fields worked and turned or hayed and mowed or resting fallow under a snowy blanket, animals anticipating their evening feed and a night's rest. High desert sunsets were almost always spectacular and now, during the dawn of the year, they came early, the sky often fully dark by five o'clock. Chris glimpsed the gathering sunset. He figured he had about an hour left.

He bent to his work, cleaning stalls and spreading straw. Thunderheads rolling along the distant hills, together with the steadily dropping temperature, suggested there'd be snow by morning, and he wanted the animals safely and securely bedded. He had just settled Jezebel, Flossie, and their litters in the nursery barn and was turning up the methane heat in the farrowing stalls when he heard a truck pull up outside. Immediately his heart raced in anticipation.

But it wasn't Sarah. Of course it wasn't. He chided himself for even letting the thought cross his mind. What would she be doing back here, anyway? He swallowed disappointment as he went out to meet the truck.

"Hey there, White Eyes. How you been?" A tall, powerfully built man swung down from the cab, black hair gleaming. He was dressed in worn blue jeans, white western shirt, bolo tie, and a down-filled ski parka. He clamped a black Stetson on his head as he hit the ground.

"Logan! *Yah-ta-hey,* buddy!" Chris's eyes lit with pleasure as the two men clasped forearms and clapped each other on the shoulder. "Long time, no see."

"Yeah, I know. My excuse is tribal business, the

good of the People. And you? What's keeping you out of trouble? Besides pigs, I mean.''

Chris shrugged. ''Just pigs, I guess. Dull and boring.''

''You, Chris? Nah, I know you too well. So, who are the new women in your life?''

Chris grinned. ''You only *think* you know me, buddy,'' he said, but he couldn't suppress the image of a petite redhead with turquoise eyes and skin like fine porcelain. He led Logan toward the barn as he asked, ''What brings you slummin' around here?''

Logan followed, leaning on a fence rail as he watched Chris bed down a heavily pregnant sow. ''I may have a job for you, if you're interested.''

''A job?'' Chris looked up with interest. ''I don't usually do legal work.''

''Neither do I, now that you mention it. Since I accepted a retainer from the tribal council, I find I'm mostly a well-paid gofer.'' Logan forced an exaggerated grimace.

''Now you're the one who's faking.'' Chris grinned. ''You love representing the Navajo nation and you know it.''

''True, true. So, about that job?''

Chris leaned against the rail. ''Tell me more.''

Chris's Navajo friend settled comfortably. ''The issues with the *Dineh* now are what they've always been since the first Mexican settlers moved north—land and money. Some of my colleagues are working on the land issue in the courts—''

''I heard about the settlement last year,'' Chris interrupted. "More than thirty-eight thousand acres that had previously been ceded to the Hopi. Good job."

"Drop in the bucket." Logan drew a deep breath. "Anyway, my end of it is trying to bring in industries that will be compatible to life on the rez, acceptable to the People, and enriching to tribal coffers. We have a couple of ideas. One of them is raising pigs."

"Pigs? The Dineh have never raised pigs."

Logan shrugged. "I know. Even in our earlier raiding days, we mostly stole sheep, horses, and cattle. But we're not talking about raising pork for ourselves. There's a place near my dad's in Upper Greasewood where a fellow tried to raise cattle a few years back. He's got pumps and wells, so there's adequate water, plus he built corrals and shelters and the fencing is still good. The whole thing is on tribal land and the tribe can pick up the rest for a song. All we need are pigs and corn—"

"And the People have always been good at raising corn," Chris added.

"—and with some good advice, we should be able to start a serious commercial operation."

Chris began to understand and his brow furrowed. "Wait a minute. You're asking me to hire on to advise the Navajo nation about how to raise pigs so you guys can compete with me in my own market?"

Logan grinned. "You always *were* quick. But that isn't exactly what we want. We'd like to create a coop with you and the other big farms in the area—the Rays down near Snowflake, the Watsons near Winslow, a few small producers in Joseph City and Taylor.

We figure that with our combined product, we can offer more pork to larger markets, stabilize the prices, and come out with everybody ahead.''

Chris weighed the idea; there were some possibilities. ''That has potential. Keep talking, partner.''

For the next half hour, the two men worked side by side in the barns, Logan describing the tribe's plan for creating a pork industry while he helped Chris run water in troughs, wash waste from stalls, and haul grain and straw. By the time they were ready to lock up for the night, Chris was ready to investigate the idea further. ''I'd like to come out to look at the place you have in mind,'' he offered.

''I reckoned you'd say that. Maybe this coming weekend?''

Chris glanced at the lowering sky. ''Sure, if the weather's good.''

''We'll leave it that way, then,'' Logan said. ''Because of the necessary health regulations, inspections, and so forth, we'll also need to bring a good veterinarian on board,'' he said as he walked toward his pickup. ''We'd like to find someone young and energetic, who could follow the project for a while. You don't happen to know of someone?''

Chris grinned as he thought of a woman with hair like fire and a spirit to match. ''You know,'' he said, ''I just might.'' Suddenly the possibilities seemed endless.

''. . . and a difficult birth in a pig,'' Sarah said, finishing her recitation of the day's calls as she handed her father a dinner tray.

He reached for it, leaning over the leg cast he kept elevated on the seat of a chair. "Everything come out okay?" he asked with a twinkle.

Sarah wrinkled her nose at the old doctor's pun. "Yeah, it did. All fourteen piglets." She took her own tray and sat near him. "In fact, I was surprised how easy it was. Of course, the last unusual presentation I handled was in a thoroughbred mare. By comparison, the sow seemed easy." She didn't add that attending animal births, something she'd once had trouble doing, was becoming easier all the time.

"I guess it would at that," Richards answered, chuckling as he thought of her handling the mare. "Whose pig was it?"

"A brooder out at Rainbow Rock Farms."

"Ah, the McAllister place. They're good customers. Know enough about their own animals to handle most simple problems, and care enough about them to call quickly when they need veterinary help."

"You're right about that. Chris delivered another difficult birth by himself just before I got there."

"Chris?" her father asked, raising a brow. "You're already on a first-name basis?"

"It seemed easier than calling him Mr. McAllister," she answered evenly, grateful that her telltale complexion hadn't done anything foolish—like blushing.

"He was in your class in school, wasn't he?"

She resisted the urge to tell her father he was prying. "No, you're probably thinking of his brother, Kurt— and he was a year behind me. Chris was a freshman when I graduated, just a skinny little kid with lots of wild blond hair.'' She took a big bite of stir-fried cabbage and onion.

"Last I remember, he was neither skinny nor little,'' her father answered, a speculative note to his voice.

Sarah smiled indulgently, glad her full mouth gave her an excuse not to answer immediately. She swallowed. "Father dear, your thinly veiled attempts at matchmaking have been duly noted. But if you want to find someone who can settle me down, you're going to have to look elsewhere. Chris McAllister is three years younger than I am and probably not the least bit interested in an older, slightly-used model when the world is full of sweet young ones.''

"There you go, talking yourself down again.'' Doc Richards started in on his "nobody values you if you don't value yourself'' lecture and Sarah obediently half-listened, content to have dodged that bullet. But a funny thing happened as she munched on her veggies and rice.

Her mind kept conjuring unbidden images of Chris McAllister in worn jeans and a chambray work shirt, frowning in undisguised distrust of her abilities, then grinning in equally open appreciation of her work the first moment she proved him wrong. Male chauvinists she was used to; men willing to appreciate her were something else again.

She sighed. Of course he was too young for her—not just in years, but in experience, a world of experience. That didn't mean she couldn't *look*, did it?

She *had* looked, rather openly and more than once, whenever she thought Chris wouldn't notice. She'd seen how the extra-large work shirt pulled tight across his back and biceps when he dragged the hose toward her. She'd watched his thigh muscles bunch when he bent to help her, had seen the way the sunlight caught the golden hairs on his chiseled forearms.

And his face! The man had a face to make a woman's mouth water—all clean, high planes and straight angles. A high, well-formed brow led to eyes the color of thunderclouds, intelligent eyes that hinted of a world of depth and feeling. He had the same straight, patrician nose she remembered on the older McAllister boys, and the same full, sensual mouth. What she hadn't remembered on either of the other brothers were those dimples and the boyish grin that went with them. Yum! The man looked good enough to—well, to look at, anyway.

She glanced at her dad, who was still fussing about all her good, marriageable qualities, and smiled a small, secret smile. Well, marriage wasn't in the cards, but if chance favored her with another opportunity to hang around Chris McAllister, she'd make a point of looking—and enjoying whatever she saw.

Chapter Two

Pigs, huh? On the reservation? Well, maybe if they flew there . . .

Sarah downshifted and gunned her dad's truck, taking the hill with ease. She'd been pondering the idea of a commercial pig farm on Navajo land since the call from Logan Redhorse that morning. The more she thought about it, the more it made sense.

She'd taken that call on her cellular phone while traveling toward a routine visit at the Westover dairy. Her first instinct was to tell this Redhorse person, whoever he was, to stop playing games with the telephone. That's when he'd mentioned Chris McAllister. She had ended up sitting in front of the dairy for half an hour, taking notes on a brown paper bag.

Now as she headed toward home, she picked up her

phone again and called her dad. "Know anything about a man called Logan Redhorse?" she asked when he answered.

"Sure," her father said. "He's a young hotshot attorney who represents the tribal council. He called me a couple of times last year to look at cattle on the reservation. Is that where you're headed now?"

"No, not now," Sarah answered, and told him about the plans for a pig farm. His reaction was the same as everyone else's. No one had ever heard of Navajos raising pigs. Then like everyone else, he saw the wisdom of the idea. "They ought to be able to make a go of it, I'd think. There's always a market for good, corn-fed pork."

Sarah shrugged, then added, "Apparently Chris thought so."

"Chris who?"

"McAllister," she responded, mentally chiding herself for the slip. "He recommended me to Redhorse."

"You must have made quite an impression yesterday." The tone in her father's voice confirmed that she'd blown it. When her dad got an idea in his head, he was like a terrier with a rat. "If you take this deal, you'll be working fairly closely with McAllister, won't you?"

"Possibly," Sarah added, trying to sound vague. "Look, Dad, how will I handle local veterinary emergencies if I'm traveling on the reservation?"

"Same way *I* always did, I guess. Warn your clients when you're going to be away, then let them call someone else if they have a problem while you're gone. There are only a few of us who do large animal work, and we're all pretty used to covering for one another.''

Sarah mentally checked that problem off her worry list. ''Sounds like maybe I ought to check it out,'' she said.

''Especially if you'll be working with that handsome McAllister boy,'' her dad offered.

Sarah said good-bye quickly and blew out a slow sigh. Might as well admit it to herself, if not to her dad. Chris McAllister was one of the project's main attractions. As she took the road north from Holbrook, she realized she was within a couple of miles of Rainbow Rock Farms, and had nearly two hours to go until her next appointment. The call from Logan Redhorse would give her an excuse to drop in. Only she would know her real reason for stopping—to see whether ''that handsome McAllister boy'' was really as attractive as she remembered.

She couldn't be as attractive as he remembered, Chris assured himself as he poured silage and mash into the feed troughs in the nursery barn, his memory crowded with visions of the red-haired dynamo who had blown in here yesterday. Hurricane Sarah had certainly taken the farm by storm. ''But she wasn't really *that* great, was she, Flossie?'' he asked the pig he was feeding, who grunted a satisfied reply. He rubbed the animal's ears. ''Oh, what would you know? You're prejudiced.'' Flossie grunted in pleased response.

Chris laughed aloud, then let his mind linger on the

memories and images that had been haunting him
since Sarah's arrival yesterday, even in his sleep. He
wondered if she could actually have been as tiny as
he'd thought, probably not over five-three. She was
little around the middle, too. He figured he could almost span her waist with his two outstretched hands—
that is, assuming she'd let him touch her. He chuckled
at that. The lady would probably knock him into next
Christmas if he laid a finger on her anywhere, and
that's just what he had been thinking of doing ever
since he'd seen the milky whiteness of her skin. Small
she might be, but he imagined that if he ever held her,
his arms would be full of woman. The thought made
his skin tingle.

"Daydreaming?"

He whirled, surprised by the voice. Sarah McGill
appeared in the doorway and he wondered for a moment if he'd conjured her out of thin air.

She broke the silence. "Sorry if I startled you."

"N-no problem," Chris stammered, then added,
"What can I do for you, Doc?"

"It's what you've already done for me, *Goldie*."

Chris winced. "Ouch. I thought we'd gotten past
that."

"You started it."

"I what?" Then he understood. "Oh, the doc
crack."

"Yeah, the doc crack." She came closer, leaning
on the fence rail just a few feet away from him, close
enough for him to smell her soft, slightly floral scent,
close enough he could see the expression in her

vivid turquoise eyes. The more he saw, the better he liked it.

"I had a call this morning from Logan Redhorse," she began.

"Ah, the Copper Crusader."

"What?" Sarah drew back in distaste.

"He used to call himself that when we were in college together. The Copper Crusader, the Bronze Bomber—he was always making light of his native ancestry, but dead serious about fighting for the rights of his people."

Sarah shook her head. "Seems like an interesting guy."

A sliver of jealousy knifed through Chris. Why couldn't she find *him* interesting? "So what do you think of the pig farm?"

"That's what I wanted to ask you. You're the expert on commercial hog operations," she said, and Chris warmed at her approval. "Do you think they stand a chance?"

It suddenly seemed very important to him to appear as an expert. He furrowed his brow. "Well, it depends."

"On . . . ?" she prodded.

"On a host of things. Most of us operate near our margin just to stay in business. It's never easy to turn out a quality product and sell at a pittance, but the proposition becomes even more iffy when it has to depend on things like weather and corn crops, the price of diesel for shipping, changes in government regulations—"

She cut him off. "I see what you mean."

"All in all, I'd say they stand as good a chance of making it as any of us, especially if they get a co-op going."

"The co-op sounded like a good idea to me. Are you in? I mean, assuming they get it going?"

"It's an all-or-nothing proposition for me," Chris answered. "I'm in the whole way or not at all."

"That makes sense."

"What about you, Doc? I mean, Dr. McGill?"

She grinned. "Sarah will do."

His voice softened and he leaned slightly toward her. "What about you, Sarah?"

Her eyes softened in equal measure and lingered, if only for a second, on his mouth. Her own lips felt quivery. "I think I'd like to see what they have planned before I commit to anything."

"Me, too. Weather permitting, I'm planning to meet Logan at the corrals near Upper Greasewood next Saturday around eleven. If you'd like, you can ride along."

Sarah barely debated. "I'd like."

Chris felt warm all over. "I'll pick you up at your place a little before ten, then. That's assuming you're staying with your dad."

"That's right, but make it nine-thirty. Those roads are likely to be slower than usual if we get the storm that's threatening." The sadness lingered about her again, out of proportion to the threat of a coming storm.

rvelous, in fact. But he's a kid, Eden, not
than your baby brother.''

ther is barely eighteen, Sarah. Don't tell
robbing the cradle these days?''

t hardly. I guess he's a *little* older than Rob-

much older?''

t know. He was three years behind me in
that probably makes him—''

ty-six,'' Eden finished. ''Sounds like fair
ne.''

'm not hunting, and I'm not robbing cradles,
ou'd have to meet him to see what I mean,
older than he is, Eden, and I'm not just talk-
t the calendar. Chris is so much younger—''

s, huh? Nice name.''

h, well, he's all wrong for me.''

ch of us are you trying to persuade, you or

sighed. ''Good question.''

you seeing him soon?''

morrow. We're going out to the reservation to
ut a site for a pig farm. If everything goes as
d, we may be working together for a while,
the Navajo nation get into production.''

unds like a fine excuse to spend some time to-
''

guess we'll see.'' Sarah kept the conversation on
erful note until she finally said good-bye, but
as she pulled in beside the home she shared with
d, she wondered why everyone—well, everyone

''Sounds good.'' He tried to make his smile encouraging.

''How long do you think we'll be gone?''

He shrugged. ''Mid-afternoon or later, I'd guess.
Why?''

''I was wondering if I should throw some sandwiches in a bag or something.'' She colored slightly
and looked away as she said it, and Chris understood
that she was trying to downplay anything that smacked
of a social connection.

Still, picnicking with Sarah McGill had merit.
''That's probably a good idea,'' he said seriously,
''only let me take care of it. I can pick up some
chicken and fixings. We'll call it a business lunch and
invite Logan to join us. Maybe he'll let us warm the
food at his dad's place.''

Sarah looked relieved. ''Sounds good. I'll see you
Saturday, then.''

''Nine-thirty,'' he confirmed.

She flashed him a bright smile as she left and Chris
found himself staring at an empty space where she had
just stood. He thought of the long ride alone with her
on Saturday and felt more eager anticipation than he'd
felt about anything since he was a kid looking forward
to Christmas. One thing was certain: she was at least
as attractive as he had remembered.

The storm came, powdering the high desert with
several inches of snow and dropping the temperatures
below the zero mark, but by Friday afternoon the skies
were clearing, the sun was shining, and the melt-off

had begun. Sarah scanned the sky, pleased that good weather would permit the trip to the reservation tomorrow. She was looking forward to it more than she wanted to admit. "That handsome young cowboy" her father kept pushing at her was every bit as gorgeous as she had remembered.

Humming lightly to herself, Sarah climbed into the cab of her father's veterinary truck and started toward home. Then on a whim, she picked up the cellular phone and dialed the number for The Old Woman's Shoe in Phoenix. When a bright voice answered, Sarah asked for Eden Grant.

"Just a moment, please," the woman said, and put her on hold.

Sarah waited, pondering how much this waiting time must be costing her, and not really caring. It had been long enough since she and Eden had chatted. Moments later, Eden answered. "Sarah! How lovely to hear from you. To what do I owe this honor?"

"Nothing, really," Sarah answered. "I guess I just wanted to hear your voice. How are things in Phoenix?"

"Sunny. Warm. Noisy around all these kids. Lonely without you in the apartment. How are things in your dad's veterinary practice?"

"Good. I'm getting lots of practice with all kinds of problems that I never would have seen at the racetrack."

Eden's voice warmed. "Then I guess it's a good thing that your dad broke his knee and kept you from taking that cushy job with the horses—"

"—or that great

in.

"—or the sexy n
finished.

"Yeah, I rememb
voice oozed sarcasm
lucky to have a dad v

"Yes, you are," E
serious than Sarah's. "
have a dad, whether he

"I know, Eden. Sorr
ciative. I guess I just ha
here the last few days."

"Well, chin up. The
from what I hear. Beside
to your being there that y
mean, that condo in Scotts
that comes equipped with I

Sarah laughed. "No, I d

"So have you met anyor
Sarah hesitated a beat
really."

"Don't kid me. I can hear
quickly. I'll bet he's another

Sarah sighed. "Tall, defin
or so. Rangy, no. This guy is
blocks aren't as well built. As
raises pigs."

"Close enough," Eden decla
terrific in boots and jeans."

"Terrific," Sarah agreed, a

voice. "Ma
much older

"My br
me you're

"No, n
bie—"

"How
"I don
school, so

"Twen
game to

"But I
either. Y
but I *am*
ing abou

"Chri
"Yea
"Wh
me?"

Sarah

"Are

"To
check
planne
helpin

"S
gethe

"I
a che
later,
her d

but herself—seemed to think she and Chris would make such a good match.

"Sounds like a perfect match," Kate McAllister was saying. She had just returned from Joan and Bob's house and now sat in the kitchen with her youngest son, chatting over a cup of coffee. Chris had been telling her about the Navajo plan to raise pigs commercially. "We know they have feeding pens and plenty of corn," she said. "If they've found a place with enough water, I'd say they've got the potential of putting us right out of business."

"A farmers' co-op is part of the plan," Chris explained, and went on to tell his mother about the co-operative as Logan had outlined it.

"That Logan is a bright one," she answered, shaking her head thoughtfully. "I always liked him."

"He likes you, too," Chris answered, "and that makes you a rarity. He's not partial to *belagaana* women."

Kate shrugged. "He was always difficult to please, but he's a nice young man. Nice-looking, too. I'm sure there are *some* Anglo women who appeal to him."

Chris shrugged. "Women, plenty, but not very many Anglo women."

Kate shrugged. "So when will you talk with him again?"

"Tomorrow. We're going out to the rez to check out the place where he wants to set up."

"We? You and Logan?"

''We'll be meeting Logan out there. I'm taking a vet with me, another potential adviser to the project.''

Kate noticed her son did not meet her eyes. ''Tell me about this vet,'' she said, her voice heavy with suggestion.

How does she always know? Chris wondered. He stalled with another sip of coffee. ''Name's Sarah McGill,'' he said. ''Used to be Sarah Richards. She's filling in for her dad while he recovers from an injury.''

''Wiley's hurt? Nothing serious, I hope?''

''A broken kneecap. One of his patients kicked him.''

''Ouch.'' Kate winced. ''Occupational hazard, I guess.''

''Suppose so.'' Chris took another big swallow.

''So this Sarah is his daughter?''

He tried to contain his sigh. He had hoped they'd dropped that topic. ''Yeah. She just got her veterinary degree last year.''

''She must be the one who married that rodeo rider,'' Kate mused, her eyebrows drawn together, ''the guy who got stomped to death in Cheyenne.''

Chris felt again that sensation of being kicked in the stomach, only this time it wasn't at all pleasant. ''Stomped to death?''

''If I remember correctly. He was riding for the championship, only he lost his grip early. The bull threw him, then turned and stomped him. By the time the rodeo clowns could distract the bull and get the rider out of the ring, it was too late.''

''And he was married to Sarah?''

"Sounds good." He tried to make his smile encouraging.

"How long do you think we'll be gone?"

He shrugged. "Mid-afternoon or later, I'd guess. Why?"

"I was wondering if I should throw some sandwiches in a bag or something." She colored slightly and looked away as she said it, and Chris understood that she was trying to downplay anything that smacked of a social connection.

Still, picnicking with Sarah McGill had merit. "That's probably a good idea," he said seriously, "only let me take care of it. I can pick up some chicken and fixings. We'll call it a business lunch and invite Logan to join us. Maybe he'll let us warm the food at his dad's place."

Sarah looked relieved. "Sounds good. I'll see you Saturday, then."

"Nine-thirty," he confirmed.

She flashed him a bright smile as she left and Chris found himself staring at an empty space where she had just stood. He thought of the long ride alone with her on Saturday and felt more eager anticipation than he'd felt about anything since he was a kid looking forward to Christmas. One thing was certain: she was at least as attractive as he had remembered.

The storm came, powdering the high desert with several inches of snow and dropping the temperatures below the zero mark, but by Friday afternoon the skies were clearing, the sun was shining, and the melt-off had begun. Sarah scanned the sky, pleased that good weather would permit the trip to the reservation tomorrow. She was looking forward to it more than she wanted to admit. "That handsome young cowboy" her father kept pushing at her was every bit as gorgeous as she had remembered.

Humming lightly to herself, Sarah climbed into the cab of her father's veterinary truck and started toward home. Then on a whim, she picked up the cellular phone and dialed the number for The Old Woman's Shoe in Phoenix. When a bright voice answered, Sarah asked for Eden Grant.

"Just a moment, please," the woman said, and put her on hold.

Sarah waited, pondering how much this waiting time must be costing her, and not really caring. It had been long enough since she and Eden had chatted. Moments later, Eden answered. "Sarah! How lovely to hear from you. To what do I owe this honor?"

"Nothing, really," Sarah answered. "I guess I just wanted to hear your voice. How are things in Phoenix?"

"Sunny. Warm. Noisy around all these kids. Lonely without you in the apartment. How are things in your dad's veterinary practice?"

"Good. I'm getting lots of practice with all kinds of problems that I never would have seen at the racetrack."

Eden's voice warmed. "Then I guess it's a good thing that your dad broke his knee and kept you from taking that cushy job with the horses—"

"—or that great Scottsdale condo—" Sarah chimed in.

"—or the sexy neighbor who came with it," Eden finished.

"Yeah, I remember him." Sarah sighed, and her voice oozed sarcasm when she added, "I sure am lucky to have a dad who needs me."

"Yes, you are," Eden answered, her voice more serious than Sarah's. "You know I'd give anything to have a dad, whether he needed me or not."

"I know, Eden. Sorry I'm not feeling more appreciative. I guess I just have the blues. It's been stormy here the last few days."

"Well, chin up. The weather should be improving from what I hear. Besides, there might be advantages to your being there that you haven't told me about. I mean, that condo in Scottsdale can't be the only place that comes equipped with hot-and-cold running men."

Sarah laughed. "No, I don't suppose it can."

"So have you met anyone interesting?"

Sarah hesitated a beat before saying, "No, not really."

"Don't kid me. I can hear it in your voice. So tell, quickly. I'll bet he's another tall, rangy cowboy."

Sarah sighed. "Tall, definitely—probably six-two or so. Rangy, no. This guy is solid muscle. Some city blocks aren't as well built. As for the cowboy part, he raises pigs."

"Close enough," Eden declared. "I'll bet he looks terrific in boots and jeans."

"Terrific," Sarah agreed, a wistful note in her

voice. "Marvelous, in fact. But he's a kid, Eden, not much older than your baby brother."

"My brother is barely eighteen, Sarah. Don't tell me you're robbing the cradle these days?"

"No, not hardly. I guess he's a *little* older than Robbie—"

"How much older?"

"I don't know. He was three years behind me in school, so that probably makes him—"

"Twenty-six," Eden finished. "Sounds like fair game to me."

"But I'm not hunting, and I'm not robbing cradles, either. You'd have to meet him to see what I mean, but I *am* older than he is, Eden, and I'm not just talking about the calendar. Chris is so much younger—"

"Chris, huh? Nice name."

"Yeah, well, he's all wrong for me."

"Which of us are you trying to persuade, you or me?"

Sarah sighed. "Good question."

"Are you seeing him soon?"

"Tomorrow. We're going out to the reservation to check out a site for a pig farm. If everything goes as planned, we may be working together for a while, helping the Navajo nation get into production."

"Sounds like a fine excuse to spend some time together."

"I guess we'll see." Sarah kept the conversation on a cheerful note until she finally said good-bye, but later, as she pulled in beside the home she shared with her dad, she wondered why everyone—well, everyone

Kate flashed an inquiring look, but kept the thought to herself. "Um-hm. She was just out of high school when they were married, and they couldn't have been together more than a year or two. She must have been a very young widow."

Widow. Chris winced at the word. He'd always connected it with bent, gray-haired old crones—not redheaded dynamos. Not Sarah. The sadness he sometimes felt around her suddenly made sense. "That must have been tough for her." He swallowed the last of his sentence with his coffee.

"Yes." Kate stretched and leaned back in her chair, then caught sight of the two plastic-wrapped chickens thawing on the counter. "You're cooking?"

"For tomorrow. Thought I'd take a lunch out to the rez for Logan and Sarah and me."

Kate's eyes widened. "And you're cooking it *yourself*?"

Chris shrugged. "Seemed like a good idea at the time."

Kate grinned, her eyes sparkling with mischief. "Sarah Richards was always a pretty girl."

Chris opened his mouth to answer, then thought better of it and closed it again. He walked away, shaking his head, while his mother chuckled behind him.

"The fence seems sturdy enough." Sarah leaned against the corral by the roadside in Upper Greasewood, trying to rock the fence that stood as if made of stone.

Chris suppressed a grin. Sarah's light weight wasn't

about to rock this fence. He must weigh half again what she did. "Let me try it," he said, throwing his shoulders into a giant shove. The corral stood immovable. "Feels solid to me," he concluded, rubbing a sore shoulder. The fence was plenty solid, and built for utility, not looks, its rails on the inside to thwart the efforts of any cattle that might have learned to lean on the side boards, pushing them until the nails came free.

"It wouldn't hold pigs, though," Sarah said, looking at Logan.

"No, we realize that. The plan is to run four-foot hogwire around the inside of every fence railing."

"That would do it, all right." Sarah turned her eyes toward the barns in intense inspection.

Chris was inspecting her instead, his eyes returning to her hair, her face, her slim, strong body every time she looked away. It had been a pleasant ride out that morning. He had entertained her with his memories of her performance as Maylilly Dilly in the senior class play. She'd lisped and spat to spurn the affections of the man doomed to wed her so that she might pursue a face she'd once seen on a bus. The play had been a farce, almost too silly to recall, but he had never forgotten Sarah's role in it, or the dynamic and highly sensual energy she had been able to project clear to the back of the auditorium. So this morning he had been well prepared to laugh and joke about Maylilly, the questions he had really wanted to ask hanging like cobwebs in the air about them.

"Shall we have a look at the barns?" Sarah asked,

and both men willingly followed her. It took them only a short while to conclude that, although sized for larger animals, the barns and sheds would be well suited to the purpose of raising hogs. Here and there an extra panel would be hung over a doorway or a half-open wall to provide extra shade for the pigs, who, like humans, sunburned if they stayed in the open too long. Except for that, the stalls, aisles, and corrals were well positioned to create places for farrowing and nursing the young, separating weanlings from their mothers, and fattening the older pigs for market.

"I'd say you have a good setup here, Logan," Sarah concluded as they left the larger building. "What do you think, Chris?"

"Hm?" Caught daydreaming, with his thoughts of Sarah and the man she had married, he'd forgotten to follow the thread of the conversation.

"The barns," she repeated. "It looks to me like they have a good setup for a commercial hog farm. I wonder if you agree."

"Yes," Chris said, remembering to play the expert. "Looks good to me, Logan. You may soon be in business, buddy."

"That's our next topic, White Eyes." Logan clapped him on the shoulder. "We're going to need breeding stock to start us off. What have you got for us?"

"Me?" Chris felt like kicking himself. He should have anticipated this. Too engrossed in other thoughts, he had let business slide—and Logan had caught him off guard. He really was going to have to get his thoughts under control. "I think we can come up with something," he stalled.

"Let's go on back to my dad's place and sit down over a cup of something warm," Logan said, toeing his boot into a snowdrift as he spoke. "We'll get out some paper and pens and see if we can come to an agreement we can both live with."

"Sounds good," Chris said. "I brought lunch. Maybe we can warm it at your dad's place."

"Sounds good," Logan repeated.

An hour later, they sat at a Formica dining table in a single-wide mobile home, the chicken warming in the oven, the three of them warming over a pot of steaming coffee. Logan's father, Albert Redhorse, was traveling on the New Mexico side of the reservation, so they had the place to themselves. Chris looked at the figures they had sketched on a yellow legal pad, still chiding himself for all he had not anticipated. If he'd given himself a chance to think this through, he might have been better prepared.

"Looks like we have a deal, then," Logan was saying, and Chris only nodded with a noncommittal "uh-hm." Logan continued, "You'll keep eight young sows for us out of the crop you're fattening for market right now, ones whose mothers have been top brooders. In three months, we'll be set up to move them in."

"Do you think you can acquire the others you'll need?" Chris asked, a little abashed at the small dollar figure he'd settled for.

"We targeted five places to work with," Logan said. "We're asking for eight sows from each. So far, we've had good cooperation."

"You mean you've already talked to others?" Chris didn't know whether he felt more surprised or hurt. He had expected an inside track.

"Three others," Logan said. "I knew you were coming out this weekend, so I waited to talk to you until you were here." He paused, seeming to read Chris's expression. "None of the other hog farmers are working with us as advisers," he added.

Chris nodded. "Makes sense."

Logan went on, "We'll go to the Rays next week. If they also agree, we'll be prepared to start with forty sows by the time the place is fixed up."

"That sounds workable," Chris said, his voice flat.

Sarah cleared her throat, looked at her watch, then turned pointedly to Logan. "Do you think that chicken is warm yet?"

Chris picked up her cues. "Are you in a hurry to get back?"

"I do have one appointment I need to keep this afternoon," she answered.

"We'd better get moving, then." Chris stood and went to the oven where his pan-fried chicken was now steaming. He sympathized. He'd felt the same way every time Sarah had looked at him all morning. "It looks good enough to eat," he concluded, waving the steaming pan in front of them.

"Smells great, too." Sarah looked at her watch again. "I hate to run and eat," she said, "but do you think we could leave some lunch with Logan, then hit the road with the rest?''

Chris turned to his friend. ''Okay with you?''

''Just leave me plenty when you go,'' Logan answered, making a show of rubbing his stomach.

''I thought your dad would be here, so I have plenty extra,'' Chris said, helping himself to a chipped plate from the small kitchen cupboard and pushing off four large pieces. He opened the refrigerator and shoveled out large helpings of potato and three-bean salad, topped it off with a helping of chocolate cake, then repacked everything to go.

''Are you ready to leave?'' he asked Sarah.

She returned an amiable smile. ''Any time you are.''

They said their quick good-byes and left Logan standing in the doorway waving as they drove the truck away. Minutes later they were back on the road toward Rainbow Rock.

''What time is your appointment?'' Chris asked as he checked his watch.

Sarah ducked her head as a coy expression stole over her face. ''I have a confession,'' she said. ''I don't really have an appointment.''

''No?'' Chris's face mirrored his confusion.

''No,'' she answered. ''That is, unless *you're* the appointment.''

''What—?''

''I wanted to talk to you alone,'' she said.

Chris stared at her as the pickup slowed to a crawl.

Chapter Three

Sarah realized she'd just shot the concentration of her driver. "Look," she said, "I didn't mean to shake you up. Why don't you find a place to pull off the road? We can get out your lunch while it's still hot."

Chris's voice was husky, and contained no small degree of suspicion. "I thought you wanted to talk."

"I do, but it's nothing that can't be said over food."

"It just can't be said in front of Logan," Chris clarified.

Sarah gave him a long, patient look. "Let's say it isn't really Logan's business." She reached behind the seat for the picnic basket. "Come on, pull over while I get the food out."

"Okay." He put his hand on her arm. "Look, why don't you wait on that? There's a pullout about eight miles down the road that has a nice view. I'll help you with the food when we get there.''

"Okay," Sarah agreed, and rested against the back of the seat.

She wanted to talk to him alone? Something that wasn't Logan's business? Chris tried to run the possibilities through his mind as they drove rapidly down the narrow, two-lane road. He tried, but he couldn't find any that made sense. What was going on here, anyway? It seemed to take a very long time to cover the eight miles to the pullout, especially since they traveled in tense silence. When they got there, the bright red gash in the earth that made such a lovely view from this spot was buried in snow. So much for romantic ambience. "Looks like we're here." Chris stopped the truck and set the brake, then reached behind the seat and lifted their picnic box into the space between them.

"The chicken's still hot," Sarah observed as she set out two paper plates, then removed the foil covering.

"I cooked it myself, you know."

Sarah looked impressed. "Really? I may have to try some."

"You weren't planning to?"

"I don't usually."

Chris pulled back. "Oh, no. Don't tell me you're vegetarian." His expression suggested he'd be more eager to lunch with an ax murderer.

She laughed. "Would that be so bad?"

"Only to a family that raises meat for a living."

"I hadn't thought of that." Sarah took a piece of

chicken for herself. "But to reassure you, no, I'm not vegetarian—not as a matter of moral commitment, anyway. I've just learned from experience that I usually feel better when I avoid meat and dairy products."

Chris stared. "Avoid? As in, completely?"

Again she laughed. "Don't worry. I love a rib-eye steak—or a barbecued pork loin—as much as the next person. I just don't indulge very often. I feel better that way."

"So what do you eat?" he asked. Chris had never been able to fathom how people could eat meal after meal without meat in it.

"Everything else," Sarah answered simply. "The potato and rice and vegetable dishes that other people serve as side dishes with their meat main course. I just eat them without the meat." She dished up tiny portions of the two salads and passed the bowls to him, her expression growing more serious. "Listen, Chris, I didn't lure you out here to talk about food choices."

He straightened. "So why did you lure me out here?"

She met his eyes. "I saw what was happening back there. You led me to think that you and Logan are old friends, but it didn't seem that way when you two were talking. There was so much tension . . ." She let the sentence drift away as her eyes left his and turned toward the window. Then she tried again. "I had the feeling I was in the way somehow. I'm wondering if it wouldn't be wiser if I bowed out."

"You mean quit?" Chris was aghast.

"It isn't as if I'm in very deep. There are other vets

in the area, and if I'm muddying the waters for you somehow—''

''That's not it at all,'' he interrupted.

''Then what is it? You seemed so distracted back there.''

''Well, you're right about that part.'' *So what do I say now?* he asked himself, then he answered. *Heck, tell her the truth.* He lifted his eyes to face her squarely. ''The truth is—'' The words stuck in his throat. Sarah gave him a quizzical look. He cleared his throat. ''The truth is that I'm very attracted to you, Sarah McGill. *Very* attracted. I suspect I'll be distracted any time you're around.''

''Oh.'' She looked away, swallowing as if she'd just gulped down a goldfish. ''Oh. Maybe I'd better quit then.''

''Why?'' Chris turned his most charming smile on full. ''I've been the perfect gentleman, haven't I?''

''Well, yes,'' Sarah agreed, ''but if you keep on like this, you're going to be a perfectly broke gentleman, and I don't think I want to be responsible.''

She looked adorable. Chris laughed out loud. ''Why don't you let that be my problem?''

''Just so long as you understand there can't . . . there can't be anything between us.''

''Why not?''

''Oh, Chris, be reasonable. I'm so much older than you are—''

''About three years,'' he clarified. ''That's not so much older.''

''It's not just the years,'' she said. ''It's the mileage.

I've been places and done things . . .'' Sarah sighed.
"You're so young.''

Chris was a fully grown man with all the needs and
feelings that accompanied that and he felt sorely
tempted to show her so. Fighting down the temptation,
he stroked work-roughened fingertips along her jaw
and across her chin, then up the other side of her face.
"Tell me about it, Sarah,'' he said, his voice low and
comforting. "Tell me about your husband.''

She looked up, eyes wide. "You knew I was married?'' He nodded. "Wait a minute. All this distress
isn't about you feeling attracted to a married woman,
is it? Because I haven't been mar—''

"I know,'' he answered. "Mom told me.''

"Told you about Jake?''

"Was that his name? All I know is that you married
him when you were very young and you were only
together a couple of years. He was a rodeo cowboy,
killed by a rodeo bull.''

She nodded. "Some bull called Widowmaker lived
up to his name.'' She turned toward the window.

Chris swallowed. "It must have been very difficult
for you.''

"It was.'' Then she turned back. "But maybe not
for the same reasons that everyone expected.''

He raised an eyebrow. "Do you want to explain
that?''

She smiled. "No, actually. I think I've talked too
much already.''

Chris noticed that neither of them had tasted their
chicken or salad. He placed the plates carefully on the

floor, then he slid closer to Sarah, tucking a comforting arm around her. "Talk to me, Sarah," he urged, stroking her face. "Tell me about it."

She leaned into his touch. Chris saw before him a passionate young woman who had denied herself this kind of human comfort too long. He promised himself he wouldn't betray the trust she was showing by permitting him to touch her this way.

"It isn't a pretty story," she said, nearly breathless from the pleasure of Chris's fingertips on her tender skin.

"Tell me anyway," he persisted, running his thumb along her bottom lip.

"Mmm." She lifted his hand down, searching his eyes. "Do you really want to hear it?"

"Yes," he answered, somewhat surprised to realize that he did want to hear it, that he wanted to know everything there was to know about pretty, red-haired Sarah.

She studied his face, then apparently made a decision. "All right," she said, snuggling into his shoulder. "Just tell me if you want me to quit." She paused.

"Go on," Chris encouraged, lifting his hand to her face again.

She took it down. "You'll have to quit that if you want me to talk."

"Why?"

"Because I can't think when you do that." Her eyes sparkled with a kind of feverish brightness that made him believe her words.

Chris realized she was trusting him with that, too.

"Okay, then I'll quit—at least for the moment." He moved closer, winding his fingers with hers. "Now, tell me about it."

She sighed. "I was lonely for so long," she began. "One of those lonely onlys you hear about. My mother discovered she had cancer when I was still a toddler. She hung on as long as she could, but she was gone by the time I was eight years old. Dad was great, but he had the practice to build and run. I went with him sometimes on after-school or weekend calls, but I also spent a lot of time alone." She looked up as if to see whether he was still watching.

"And?" he prompted.

She smiled. "And I guess I got tired of it as I entered my teens." She interrupted herself with a derisive chuckle. "I was a real buckle bunny in those days, a major rodeo fan. A couple of the girls from school and I went to every rodeo within three hundred miles of Rainbow Rock. We could name every PRCA champion for the past ten years and tell you everyone who was ranked in the current year's competition." She looked up. "You know the PRCA, don't you?"

"The Professional Rodeo Cowboys' Association," he answered.

"Right. Anyway, that's how I met Jake, at a PRCA rodeo. I was just turning eighteen and planning on graduating in a couple of months, and a bunch of us went to a rodeo in Flagstaff to gawk at the bull riders. Jake had the best ride of the day on the meanest, highest-point bull. When he came out of the arena, I was there to greet him."

"That must have made his day," Chris observed dryly. It didn't take much imagination to picture Sarah at eighteen, turned out in tight jeans and western boots.

She shrugged. "He said it did. Turns out Jake the Snake was quite the charmer."

"Jake the Snake? Now that's appealing."

"It was then. The talk about him said he had more moves than a sidewinder." She laughed, another derisive sound. "I was foolish enough to think they were talking about his performance in the arena."

Chris stroked her hair. "I take it Jake wasn't everything you were looking for?"

"No, but we were married almost a year before I figured it out. I spent the year thinking that if I was just a better wife, better housekeeper, better . . ." She paused. "I blamed myself when things went bad between us."

Chris felt himself tensing. "He didn't . . . hurt you, did he?"

"Oh, no. Not in the way you mean, anyway. Frankly, that would have taken more attention than Jake usually showed me. He was just never there. The rodeo circuit was his first love and I came in somewhere far behind."

Chris relaxed visibly, glad that Sarah had never endured some of the terrors he had just envisioned. "Did you travel the circuit with him?"

"Once in a while, but he said it cost too much to keep me with him on the road. He was dragging in prize money worth thousands of dollars, but it cost too much—'' She cut herself off, then took a deep breath before she resumed. ''Mostly he'd just take off with a couple of the other guys. They'd work the arena all day and into the evening, then crash in some cheap flophouse for the night. He could be gone two or three weeks at a time without so much as a phone call to let me know where he was or when he'd be home again.''

''So the lonely only was lonelier than ever,'' Chris filled in, finishing the story for her.

Sarah smiled up at him, a look of surprise lighting those lovely turquoise eyes. ''Exactly. After a year or so, I decided I hadn't gotten married so I could sit home alone. I started nagging him about taking me with him, or at least coming home more often.''

''Did it help?''

She shook her head. ''It just meant that whenever he was home, we argued. I got so I'd tense up whenever I heard a car approaching our apartment. I was always afraid it might be him coming home, then afraid it might not be. I never knew what to think.''

''It must have been difficult,'' he said again. ''Okay, so tell me the rest.''

''That's it,'' she said, as if the story was finished.

''No, there's more,'' Chris persisted.

''What do you mean, there's more? It's my story, isn't it? That means I get to decide when I'm finished telling it.''

Chris turned her face up to his. ''Tell me the rest, Sarah. About when Jake died.''

He saw the pain wash through her eyes. She closed

them against his scrutiny. When she opened them again, he was still giving her that warm, trusting, soulful look. She wondered if she knew he was irresistible when he looked at her like that. But what would he think if she told him? If she really told him? "You don't want to hear it," she answered.

"But I do," he assured her. "I want to hear it all."

She looked away. "There are a few details too . . ." She searched for a word. ". . . too personal to share. If I tell you what I feel I can, will you promise not to press for the rest?"

She meant it. He could see that in her eyes. Despite the fact that he wanted her to trust him with it all, he knew he could not violate this door. She'd open it herself when she felt ready. Until then, he'd have to wait. "All right. I promise."

Sarah sighed and her eyes seemed to focus far away. "The weekend before Cheyenne, he came home," she said. "I really wanted to talk with him. I hadn't seen him for almost a month and I had . . . things I wanted to tell him. He'd only been home about three minutes when he told me he was leaving in two days to go to Cheyenne. I was hurt and angry, and I just blew. We spent the whole two days arguing and screaming at each other. I never told him—" She stopped. "On the morning he left for Wyoming, I locked myself in the bathroom and refused even to see him off or say goodbye. The last thing he said as he left was, 'I really hate this, Sarah. When I get back, we'll file for divorce.' That was his last word to me—*divorce.*"

She trembled. Chris could feel it beneath his hands.

"I shuddered when I heard it. In that very moment I had a premonition that I'd never see him again. I unlocked the bathroom and went running after him, but he was turning the corner at the end of the block by the time I got outside."

Chris felt his heart turning inside out. "Then you got word about the bull-riding accident . . ."

She nodded. "Even before his buddies called me, I knew he was dead. I'd heard a radio announcement about a tragedy during the bull riding in Cheyenne, and I knew." She held back a sob.

"And you were blaming yourself," Chris finished for her.

"At first, that's all I could do." She straightened. "Well, you wanted to hear it."

"Yes, I did. Thank you for sharing that with me, Sarah."

Her look was honest, appraising. "I don't know why I did."

"Because you know you can trust me," Chris told her, stroking her hair. "Because your better instincts tell you I won't abuse your confidence."

"Oh," she said, the mischievous twinkle returning. "I thought it was just because I'd fallen for your dimples."

He grinned, and ran his thumb across her tender lower lip again. "You'd better watch yourself, Sarah McGill," he said. "You could turn a man's head with talk like that."

"Tease," she said, capturing his hand. "And now

I think I'd better call Logan Redhorse and tell him to find another vet for his project.''

Chris stiffened his back. ''If you quit, I quit.''

She grimaced. ''Don't be difficult, cowboy. You know it's the best way to handle this.''

''I know of no such thing,'' he answered huffily, then he sobered. ''Stay, Sarah. Help us with the project. I promise to behave myself and to give more attention to my work, but I don't want you leaving on my account. You're a good vet and the project needs you. Besides, I want to spend the time with you.'' He took both her hands in his and held them against his chest. ''Stay, Sarah. Promise me you will.''

''You know I shouldn't . . .''

''Stay.''

She sighed. ''Those gorgeous dimples of yours may just be my downfall, cowboy. Okay, I'll stay. At least for now.''

He whooped for joy, then dropped a quick kiss on her lips. The look on her face suggested he'd pushed too far. ''Sorry,'' he said. ''I guess I got carried away.''

She grinned. ''If that's what happens when you're carried away, we'll have to arrange for it to happen more often.''

''I can't believe you did that.'' The long-distance reception was all Sarah's phone company had claimed it would be. Eden sounded as if she was in the same room.

''I can't believe I did, either.'' Sarah unwound the

phone cord and propped booted feet on her dad's ottoman. "I guess he seemed . . . trustworthy."

"I guess so!" Eden exclaimed. "Have you ever talked to another man about Jake? Ever in all these years?"

"Never," Sarah admitted. "It's been more than nine years since Jake died, and except for you and Dad, nobody knows what it was really like between us."

"You mean except for me, your dad, and a certain blond cowboy with great dimples."

"Correction noted."

"And then you agreed to keep working with him?"

Sarah shook her head. "Yeah. I can't believe I did that, either."

"Did you tell him about the—"

"No." Sarah cut her off quickly. "No, and I don't intend to."

"He'll need to know sometime."

"Why?"

"Sarah, he'll have to know when you two get . . . you know, closer."

"We aren't going to get closer. I'll make sure of that."

"Why not? He sounds like just what you need."

"I told you why not. I mean, he's a great kid, but—"

"Oh, stop it, Sarah." Tense silence was Sarah's only answer. Eden sighed. "Look, I know the couple of classes in child psychology that I took to run this place don't qualify me to psychoanalyze you, but if I were going to, I'd say you're distancing from this gorgeous cowboy of yours by calling him a kid. He's a grown man, easily mature enough to rev all your engines. If you haven't *noticed* that you've noticed, you're just not paying attention!''

Sarah pursed her lips for a thoughtful moment before she answered, ''You're right.''

''So you agree that your cowboy is not a kid?''

''No, I agree that you're not qualified to psychoanalyze me.''

Eden blew out an exaggerated sigh. ''What are you gaining by this tough-as-nails, I-don't-need-anyone attitude?''

Sarah considered that. ''Peace? The assurance that I'll never have to go through another relationship like the one I had with Jake?''

''True,'' Eden admitted. ''But is that worth what you're paying for it?''

Sarah wrinkled her nose. ''I think I have to go now.''

Eden adopted a conciliatory tone. ''Do you know when you'll see him again?''

''I'm doing routine checkups and vaccinations at his place next Thursday.''

''Then think about what I've said, okay? You're a beautiful, talented, caring woman with a lot of love bottled up inside of you. You can use that visit Thursday to get to know him a little better, and to let him know you. Think about it, Sarah. I don't want to see you grow old alone.''

"You're almost as old as I am, and you're still alone."

"Only because I haven't found anyone I trust the way you trust your cowboy."

"Chris," Sarah said. "His name's Chris."

"Bravo!" Eden sounded positively jubilant. "You're calling him by his name now. That's a big step, Sarah."

"You and your armchair psychology . . ."

The conciliatory tone was back. "Just give it a chance, Sarah. Chris may be everything you need to help you get over all that sadness in the past."

"I don't think so." Sarah wrinkled her brow in concentration. "If I allow myself to fall for him, I'll care about him too much to saddle him with someone like me."

"That's the most ridiculous, most exasperating, most—"

"Eden, I've gotta go. Dad's calling."

"Look, think about what I said."

"I will, but don't expect me to change my mind."

"Just give it a chance."

" 'Bye, Eden."

" 'Bye. Let me know how Thursday goes."

"Okay, okay! Good-*bye!*" Sarah punctuated the last syllable by dropping the phone in its cradle. Eden was right about Sarah letting Chris get too close to her already, but that was *all* Eden was right about. It had to be. "It has to be," she repeated aloud as she went down the hall to help her father.

*   *   *

"Well, what do you think?" Sarah's dad did a clumsy turn and stepped down hard on his walking cast, newly acquired that morning. It held. So did his hurt knee.

"Looks great, Dad. Now I'll have a heckuva time keeping you down."

"Now I don't have to stay down," her dad said, starting for the kitchen.

"Yes, you do. You heard what the doctor said. The walking cast is to allow you to move around when you *need* to. The more time you spend with that leg up, the faster it's likely to heal."

"And the sooner you'll have to haul me off to a loony bin somewhere. I know you have my best interests at heart, daughter, but I'm used to an active life and all this sitting around is making me stir-crazy. What calls do you have scheduled this afternoon? Maybe I'll invite myself along."

"Dad, you're not up to tha—"

"Don't argue with me, Sarah. What calls?"

She sighed. She'd always heard that doctors made the worst patients; now she could testify to it. "I'm gelding Henry Gibson's stallion at one, and I'll only let you ride along on that one if you promise to stay behind the fence."

"That's reasonable," he agreed. "With this thing on my leg, I'd only be in the way, anyhow."

"My thoughts exactly." Sarah gave him a sidelong look. "When I'm done there, I have some routine checkups and vaccinations to do at Rainbow Rock Farms."

"The McAllister place," her father said, his expression thoughtful.

"Right," Sarah answered. She expected him to launch into another high-pressure sales pitch for why she should spend more time with "that handsome McAllister boy." Between him and Eden, she'd heard Chris's name almost as often as she'd thought it during the four days since she'd seen him last. She decided to short-circuit the sales pitch. "You can ride along on that one, too, though I won't want you trying to keep up while I make rounds."

"No, I don't think I'd keep up very well," he agreed, but he wasn't looking at her, and he didn't say a word about Chris McAllister. His lips were pursed in concentration and he seemed preoccupied.

"Are you all right?" Sarah asked.

"Hm?" He looked up as if he hadn't heard her.

"I asked if you're all right."

"Oh, yes. Just fine. I think I'd better change my shirt before we go out, though." He started toward his room.

"Change your shirt? You put it on clean two hours ago. And why do you need a clean shirt to watch me geld a horse?"

He murmured something unintelligible as he clumped his way down the hall. A minute later, Sarah heard him whistling as he stumped about his room and rummaged in the closet.

"I wonder what's gotten into him?" she asked aloud. The tuneless whistling from the other room was her only answer.

*   *   *

"Something smells good in here," Chris said as he entered his mother's kitchen. "Mom, have you been baking?"

"Fresh, hot gingerbread," she answered, lifting the pan from the oven. "I've made lemonade, too, and fresh coffee."

Chris raised an eyebrow. "What's the occasion?"

"Isn't it this afternoon that that pretty, red-haired vet makes her rounds?"

He chuckled, shaking his head. "Mother dear, you are absolutely transparent. You've already got Joan and Jim making grandchildren. With Kurt newly married, he'll be in production before long. Why are you in such a hurry to pair me off?"

"Let's just say I want to see you happily settled."

"You know better than that. I'm the baby of the family, the hopeless flirt, the confirmed bachel—"

"The one who most needs a good woman with an understanding heart and a mind as sharp as her wit," Kate said, effectively silencing his protest. "You can fool some of the people some of the time, son, but you—"

"...can't fool the mother who knows you better than you know yourself," Chris finished with her.

"That's right," she responded, "even if you *have* heard it before."

"Thanks for the goodies, anyway," Chris said as he picked up his work gloves. "I doubt we'll have an occasion to use them, but it was nice of you to think of it."

"Don't write it off too quickly." Kate got out a box of powdered sugar and began to sift it over the hot gingerbread. "She's probably had a big day out working in the corrals. It's only neighborly to invite her in for a minute."

Chris smiled. "You're really something, Mom."

"And don't you forget it," she said, wagging her sifter at him.

Chris chuckled as he walked toward the barn. The one thing he hadn't admitted was how much he wanted to see Sarah again. The lady vet had really gotten under his skin, enough to make him start wondering whether he might, in fact, be getting ready to settle down.

"Whew! That's a dangerous thought," he said aloud. Then he noticed the dust plume forming at the end of the road. When he saw the veterinary truck rocking along the rutted drive, his heartbeat picked up with such obvious force that he began to wonder if ignoring Sarah might be even worse.

"Lady, you should come with a warning label," he murmured toward the approaching truck, then he crossed his arms across his chest and waited for the object of his musing to arrive.

Chapter Four

When Sarah pulled up beside the barn and saw Chris standing there like an avenging god—or a magnificent genie just loosed from his bottle—she knew Eden had been right about one other thing: Chris McAllister was definitely a full-grown man, and a splendid one at that.

His blue chambray shirt seemed almost too small for the wide expanse of chest and shoulders he had crammed into it. Work-hardened biceps strained the fabric of the chambray sleeves while well-worn, fitted blue jeans hugged slim hips and long, runner's legs. Sarah suppressed a sigh. This was no "kid" she was dealing with, and she'd probably be safer in the long run if she acknowledged that up front.

She gave her father a quick, covert glance, hoping

he hadn't noticed her staring. He hadn't. He seemed nervous and preoccupied, and Sarah made a mental note to question him about it later, when they were alone.

Chris walked toward them, greeting them with a warm smile, and she pulled the truck to a stop beside him, barely daring to recognize that her heartbeat had just picked up a fast marching cadence. *I'll need to keep it cool and professional today,* she reminded herself as she swung out of the truck. Her father clambered out the other side at the same time.

"Welcome," Chris said to Sarah. "You too, Doc Richards. Nice to see you up and about."

"Glad to be up and about," Richards answered.

"Well—" Chris began, but he was interrupted by his mother's unexpected arrival in the barnyard.

"Sarah, Wiley. How good to see you," she said to them both, but her eyes were all for the distinguished gentleman with the graying hair. "How's your knee, Wiley?"

"Fine, fine. Getting better every day. But I don't think I can keep up with Sarah while she makes her rounds. You don't happen to have a nice, comfortable place where I might sit for a bit while the young folks work?" He beamed a charming smile in Kate's direction.

"Indeed I do," she answered. "In fact, I just took a plate of hot gingerbread out of the oven, and I've got lemonade and fresh coffee in the kitchen. Will you join me?"

"Don't mind if I do."

"Here, let me help you," Kate said, as she stepped next to Doc Richards, taking his arm.

"Why, thank you, ma'am." Wiley drew her close to his side.

Chris and Sarah both stared, wide-eyed and open-mouthed, as Kate McAllister and Wiley Richards walked toward the house together, chatting like amiable old friends.

"Well, I'll be," Chris said as they entered the front door.

"Yeah," Sarah answered, too surprised for words.

"Shall we get started?" Chris pointed to the open barn door and Sarah gathered her thoughts and her things to follow.

For the next hour, they worked side by side, keeping the chatter down and the necessary talk strictly professional. Chris gave as many injections as Sarah did and tried to start a conversation about why the state required certain kinds of vaccinations to be supervised and certified by licensed vets. Sarah gave a brief, uninterested answer about the importance of preventing certain kinds of diseases in the general animal population. All the while her mind was running at top speed, filled with wonder at the surprising new complication of her father's sudden interest in Chris's mom. *This will definitely make it tougher to keep him at a distance,* she thought as she packed away the last of her medical supplies. She wondered how he'd take it if she grabbed her things and sprinted for the truck.

But Chris wasn't sprinting anywhere. He sat on one end of a bale of straw and patted the empty spot beside him. "You've been working hard," he said. "Come and sit for a minute."

"Why?" she answered, all her defenses on full alert. "So you can tell all your friends how you got the lady vet in the barn?"

"Ouch." Chris winced, visibly withdrawing, and she knew she'd allowed her fears to push her too far.

"I'm sorry." She sat beside him, touching his arm in a gesture of apology. "That was rude and unnecessary." She took a deep, calming breath and let it out in a rush. "Eden says I do that deliberately to keep people at a distance. Maybe I do."

"I'll bet it works," Chris answered wryly, but he relaxed a little. "Who's Eden?"

"My friend. My best friend from forever. Our mothers were friends, so we don't even remember meeting. After my mom died, hers took me in like a second mother. I spent a lot of afternoons playing at Eden's house while our dads were at work. When we were in high school, her mom died, too—traffic accident. After that, we pretty much relied on each other."

"Was she one of the buckle bunnies who followed the rodeo circuit?"

"Um-hm."

"So she knew about Jake."

Sarah nodded. "She was there when I met him, there while I dated him. She stood up with me when I married him, and beside me when I buried him. She and Dad were the only ones . . ." She paused, smiling shyly. ". . . until last Saturday, she and Dad were the only ones who knew what that marriage really was."

"Sounds like a good friend." Chris relaxed a little more, putting his arm behind Sarah on the bale and leaning nearer.

"She always has been."

"And is Eden comfortably settled now with a husband and a houseful of kids?"

"Well, she has the kids. Dozens of them."

Chris cocked a brow.

"She runs a day-care center."

He chuckled. "Oh. No husband?"

"Nope. My experience made her hesitant. Eden's a beautiful woman with many admirers, but she never lets anyone get close. She keeps saying she hasn't found the right guy, but she's really afraid of finding anyone."

Chris smiled knowingly. "Sounds like someone else I know."

Sarah made a face, but chose to ignore his comment. "I've been thinking I ought to find her a nice guy and set her up with him."

Chris shook his head. "Let Cupid and the Fates worry about Eden. You've got Sarah to think about. So, what constitutes a nice guy?" He was closer now, and there was little doubt what he was thinking.

Sarah withdrew a little. "Look, Chris . . ." She licked her lips, not quite ready to meet his eyes.

"Ah, here comes the gentle-but-firm rejection." He sighed and moved his arm away. "You're going to tell me how I'm too young for you, not your type, how you're so much older and more experienced, how there can never be anything between us . . . Let's see, did I forget anything?''

The mocking tone was harsh, but his smile, still gentle, softened it. Sarah, disarmed, couldn't help but smile back. ''No, I think that's about it.''

''Why, Sarah?'' He took her by both shoulders and gently turned her to him, his handsome, perfect face filled with sincerity. ''Don't you think it's a little unfair to judge me by a standard set by some other man?''

His gaze was so intense, Sarah had to look away. ''I'm sorry. Maybe you're right, but there are—'' She looked up. ''There are things you still don't know, Chris. I'm not able to make commitments, not able to get . . .'' She swallowed. ''. . . not able to get . . . close to anyone in meaningful ways. Really, it's better if we just admit from the start that there can't be anything between us, and let it go. Trust me on this.''

Chris still held her, scrutinizing her face with that same hard intensity that had made her shrug away before. For a moment, they just looked at each other, then he dropped his hands. ''Okay,'' he said. ''We'll go with that, at least for now, but there's something we can still be to each other.''

Sarah was hesitant. ''What's that?''

''Friends,'' he said, his smile beseeching.

''Friends?''

''Yeah, friends. Like you and Eden. I'm sure you've had other friends, too.''

Sarah considered that. ''Sure, just never any guys.''

"You never had male friends?"

She shook her head. "You know what it's like growing up in Rainbow Rock. If I said hi to a boy in the hallway, the whole school knew we were 'going out' by the end of the day."

Chris grinned. "I remember. That's why my older brothers did most of their dating out of town, at least until they met their wives."

Sarah couldn't resist asking, "Are they happy?"

"Frighteningly so. It'd scare you to see it." Chris pursed his lips. "Hey, maybe that's a good idea. Jim and Meg are back in town now with their little girl, and Kurt and Alexa will be home from their honeymoon by the weekend. Everyone will be here for the family dinner on Sunday. Why don't you come out with me?" He lifted both arms in a hands-off gesture. "Strictly friends. Come to dinner on Sunday and meet my family. I guarantee you'll like Meg and Alexa, and my sister, Joan." He nodded toward the house. "We can bring your dad, too."

Sarah looked toward the house. "That's amazing, isn't it—your mom and my dad."

Chris nodded. "I'm surprised, but I think it's great."

Sarah looked thoughtful. "I guess we'll have to see what happens."

"Dinner Sunday?" Chris pressed.

She smiled. "Sure, friend." She offered her hand.

Chris took it in both of his in a firm, reassuring grip. "I'll see you Sunday then."

"I'll bring Dad out right after church."

"Okay." He looked toward the house. "Well, shall we go see how the older generation is faring?"

"Maybe we'd better check up on them," Sarah answered.

Chris laughed as he helped her up off the straw. Side by side, they walked toward the house.

More laughter greeted them at the front door—her father's with his mother's, blending in rich harmony. They followed it to the kitchen where they found Kate and Wiley chatting over gingerbread and coffee, and laughing as if they'd never heard anything so funny.

"Dare I ask?" Chris said as they entered.

"It was . . ." Kate laughed again. "It was something you said when you were little."

"Uh-oh," Chris responded. "Let's get out while the gettin's good." He took Sarah's elbow.

"Oh, no, wait. She'll want to hear this." Kate had to catch her breath before she could go on. Chris took advantage of the moment to murmur an apology in Sarah's ear, for whatever his mother was about to say. "He was probably about two," Kate began, "maybe two and a half. He and his father were getting breakfast in the kitchen that morning when Chris announced his discovery that Joan and Mommy were both girls. Jim said, 'No, hon. Mommy's a woman.' After that, Chris went around the house for days, declaring to anyone who came near, 'Mommy's a WO-man!' He had such a deep voice for a toddler, and he'd get this funny look on his face, and . . ." She collapsed in hysterical laughter again, and Wiley joined her, throwing back his head and hee-hawing.

Despite herself, Sarah couldn't help but chuckle. She tossed a mischievous look at Chris. "You've gotta admit it's kind of cute."

Chris shook his head in mock disgust. "How long do I have to live to outgrow this stuff?"

"I don't think you ever do," Sarah answered. "At least, not as long as you have parents around to remind you of it."

Chris nodded thoughtfully. "In that case, I guess I'm in no hurry."

Sarah sobered. "I know what you mean." They stood in the kitchen doorway, watching their parents laugh together, enjoying the fact that they were so obviously enjoying each other.

"Shall we let them visit for a minute?" Chris whispered toward Sarah. "Or do you have to leave?"

"No more appointments today," she whispered back. "I guess we can let this go for a while."

"Then come here for a minute. I have something to show you." Sarah followed him down the hall to a small bedroom that had been refitted as an office. He entered, then beckoned her to follow. "This is where I keep the books for the farm," he said, indicating a chair. "Logan sent me some material for the Greasewood project last week. I thought maybe you'd like to look it over."

"That sounds good," Sarah agreed, taking the chair.

Chris opened a large manila envelope and began unfolding diagrams, charts, and calculations in front of Sarah, explaining as he went. "Logan has been calculating how much corn they'll need to feed their initial crop of forty sows and their young. Here he's figured out how many litters a typical sow will drop in a year—''

''This would be for a very well-managed herd,'' Sarah said, inspecting the numbers.

''That's right,'' Chris responded, ''but we're doing that well here, and there's every reason to expect the Navajo nation can do just as well.''

''You get three-and-a-half litters from every sow, every year?''

''Right,'' he answered. ''We figure seven litters in two years is normal.''

Sarah whistled. ''That *is* good.''

Chris went on to show her Logan's estimations of how many young in each litter, how many of those sows they expected to keep for breeding, how much corn it would take to feed, then fatten, a hog from birth to market age, and so on. Sarah found the expectations high, but reasonable, and she was impressed with Logan's thoroughness and Chris's confident knowledge about his subject.

''Here he's calculated the total corn per year in bushels,'' he said, pointing to a figure, ''and here in tons.''

Sarah whistled again. ''Either way, it's a lot of corn.''

''Yeah, it is. But he thinks he can get it all. Look here.'' He turned to another chart that showed the commitments from various members of the tribe and their extended families. Again the numbers were figured both in bushels and in tons. "They have asked for less in the first year, more for each succeeding year as the herd grows. And they have commitments for a few tons more than they expect to need—just in case."

"I see," Sarah answered. "It looks like the plans are very thorough."

"I think so, too." Chris went on to show her Logan's other charts, the ones that figured such items as trucking expenses, market rates for pork, and expected investment for the tribe versus expected returns.

To Sarah, it all looked hopeful. "This seems very promising," she said, restacking the papers to put them in the envelope. "Your friend Logan is very thorough."

"Yes, he is," Chris answered.

Sarah glanced at her watch. "Gosh, look how late it is! Do you realize we've been in here more than an hour?"

Chris grinned. "Time flies when you're having fun—or spending it with a friend."

Sarah smiled back. "I did enjoy it," she answered, "but now I've really got to gather my dad and get out of here. I have stacks of paperwork to do tonight and I'll need to get dinner first."

"Then I'd better let you go," Chris said, helping her to her feet.

They found Kate and Wiley still chatting over now-cold coffee. This time their expressions were more somber and they spoke in low tones. Chris heard a mention of his father. Sarah heard it too, and flashed him a knowing look. He nodded.

"Dad?" she said gently. "It's time to hit the road."

Wiley blinked as if emerging from sleep, then looked at his watch. "Goodness! I didn't know how late it was getting."

"We've got books to do tonight," Sarah reminded him. She stepped close to help him stand and Chris jumped in beside her. Together they got Wiley to his feet. Moments later, amid a flurry of good-byes, Sarah and Wiley drove away, Chris went to the barn for evening chores, and Kate returned to her kitchen, this time to get dinner.

Another hour passed before Chris returned to the kitchen and found his mother setting out dinner and humming happily. He paused in the doorway, wondering when he had last seen her this animated.

"You had a good time today, didn't you, Mom?" he asked as he entered.

"Yes, I did." Kate tossed him a knowing smile, then continued her humming.

"So, and tell the truth now, did you really make that gingerbread for Sarah and me? Or did you know all along that Wiley was coming?"

"Let's say I hoped so," Kate answered as she put the finishing touches on the table. "I bumped into him in town last week and he told me he'd be getting his walking cast today. I mentioned that Sarah was coming out this afternoon for routine inspections, and he said he hoped he'd feel well enough to start riding along with her soon."

Chris ventured a tougher question. "So, how long have you and Wiley been—uh, friends?"

"Oh, we've known each other forever," Kate answered, not quite meeting his gaze.

Chris waited, but she didn't elaborate. "You know that's not what I'm asking, Mom. I've known Doc Richards most of my life, and I've never seen you laughing over coffee with him before."

Kate turned a mischievous smile on her son. Chris could have sworn it was the same look he'd seen this afternoon on Sarah. "Just because I'm your mother and over the hill, that doesn't mean I've stopped living."

"I didn't mean to suggest that, Mom. It's just . . . You've never seemed interested in, uh, socializing before. I mean, you've been alone a long time and you've never—"

"—had coffee with a man?"

Chris felt befuddled. "Er, something like that."

Kate laid a gentle hand on his arm. "Would it bother you if I wanted to start dating again?"

Chris felt his face warm at the word "dating," but hurried to reassure her. "No. No, not at all. It's just . . . What's changed?"

Kate sighed and set down the serving spoon she'd been holding. "Not much, I guess. And everything." She took a deep breath and started again. "When your father died, I had all I could handle just keeping the farm going and raising you kids. It was almost *more* than I could handle, and I often felt overwhelmed. If a man had shown interest then, I'd have been too harried to notice. Later, when we kind of had things worked out and moving smoothly, I was kind of used to the way things were and . . . and I guess I was afraid of rocking the boat.''

She sat in her usual place at the table and motioned Chris toward his chair. He sat, and she went on. ''Lately, I've been realizing that I've pretty much done my job around here.''

''You know we all still need you—''

''Of course I do, but not the way you once did. Joan and Jim and Kurt are all married now, and you're a grown man with a life of your own. You've studied and learned and paid attention, so I know the farm is in good hands since I turned it over to you, and you're getting higher market yields than I ever did when I ran things, higher even than we got when your father ran the place.''

''You were just getting started then,'' Chris said, uneasy with the comparison to his father.

''However it works,'' Kate went on, ''the fact is my role is changing now. I no longer have the responsibility for the family or the farm that I used to have. That's given me more time to think, to contemplate growing older, and to realize that I don't want to be alone for the rest of my life.''

Chris pondered that for a moment before he asked, ''Do you think you might want to marry Doc Richards?''

Kate turned toward her son. ''No carts before horses here, okay?''

''Okay, but do you think—''

She stopped him with a look. "Let's just wait and see how things go."

Chris accepted that as he bent his head to hear his mother say grace.

"Amen," Wiley Richards intoned, and Sarah answered, "Amen," then automatically reached to begin passing the food. The question she'd considered while she prepared their meal sat heavily on the tip of her tongue.

"So, Dad," she began. "Did you know when you asked to ride along today that you were going to spend the afternoon with Kate McAllister?"

His eyes twinkled as he said, "I hoped so."

"How long have you and Kate—?"

"We haven't. Not yet. Would it bother you if we wanted to?"

Sarah made the effort to put that together. "Wanted to . . . date each other?"

"That's what I'm asking."

"No. Why should it?"

"You just seemed uneasy with it," Wiley answered, reaching for a baked potato.

Sarah passed it to him. "Not so much uneasy as surprised, I guess. What happened? I mean, all these years you've never—"

"I know. It seems odd to me, too." He put down his fork, looking thoughtful. "I guess it's this knee injury that did it. When Diane died . . ." He saw Sarah flinch at her mother's name. "When your mother died, I was devastated. I knew I had to keep on living for your sake, but I didn't want to. If I could have wished myself into nothingness, I think I would have.''

"I know what you mean,'' Sarah murmured, remembering her own pain.

"But I couldn't just lie down and die, so I made myself too busy to think about it, to think at all. I developed the biggest large-animal practice in northern Arizona, and also spent enough time with you to assuage the guilt I felt about not being a good enough father, though that was difficult sometimes. You reminded me so much of your mom.''

Sarah rose. "Dad, don't—''

"Shh, honey. Let me say this. I know I wasn't the father I should have been. I was a good vet, but not much else. It was like all the rest of me died with her.'' He paused, his eyes growing misty. "Then I hurt my knee.''

Sarah sat back, shaking her head. "I don't understand.''

"No more sixteen- or eighteen-hour days. No more charging from appointment to appointment so fast I didn't have time to think. So I had time. So I thought.''

Wiley served more food onto his plate, then offered peas to Sarah. She answered, "No, thanks, I have some. Dad, what did you think?''

"I thought about how competent you've become, how capable of taking care of yourself. I thought about all those years that I'd spent being alone, but too busy to notice. Then I realized what my life would be like when I got too old to handle large animals anymore and had to retire, and I saw how alone I'd really be. I knew I didn't want that.''

Sarah nodded in understanding. ''So what do you think might happen between you and Kate McAllister?''

He shrugged. ''Hard to say. I guess we'll just have to wait and see. In the meantime, don't you let us old folks get in the way of you and Chris. You know I'd like to see you happily settled with a family of your own.''

''There's nothing between us, Dad. We're friends. That's all.''

''You don't look at him the way you look at your friends.''

Sarah grinned. ''Eden doesn't look that good in a pair of jeans.''

The wicked twinkle was back. ''Oh, yes, she does. You just haven't noticed.''

''Dad!''

''I'm old, but I'm not dead yet.'' He was twinkling like mad.

Sarah couldn't help herself; she grinned. Then she turned the subject back to her real concern. ''If you want to date Kate McAllister—or anyone else, for that matter—please do so, with my blessing. But don't wait for me to be 'happily settled with a family of my own.' It's not going to happen, Dad. You know it's not.''

''I know what you keep telling me, and I think it's about time you gave the possibility some thought. It's been ten years since Jake died—''

"A little over nine."

"Either way, it's long enough. You're young and healthy, you have your education behind you and a good career ahead. It's time for you to think about living."

"I *am* living, Dad, and you know that I can't . . . that I won't ever . . ." She sighed, unable to finish.

"You won't if you don't try."

Sarah dished up some carrots and passed the bowl a bit more roughly than necessary. "There's no point in discussing this," she said, filling her mouth with carrot to emphasize her point.

"Maybe not, but there's plenty of point in thinking about it."

"You think about your own love life, Dad, and let me think about mine."

"That's all I'm asking you to do, dear—think about it." Wiley Richards smiled serenely at his daughter, who wrinkled her nose, then turned her concentration to chewing carrots.

But she did think about it. She lay in bed, wide awake as images of Chris drifted through her mind, unable to think about anything else. She'd thought she had her life planned out, under control, safely protected from the kind of injuries that loving again might cause to her heart. Then an unruly horse had broken her father's kneecap and somehow, everything had changed.

"I need to be more careful, that's all," she said aloud, then turned on her side, telling herself firmly that it was time to sleep. But she didn't sleep. She just kept thinking about Sunday at the McAllister home and meeting Chris's family, about her father and Kate, about the way Chris had looked at her when he offered his friendship. She had the sensation of trying to fight her way out of quicksand, and the uncomfortable feeling that she was already in too deep to escape unscathed.

Chapter Five

Chris stood on the front porch of his family home—
the home he'd grown up in, the home he'd always
thought of as his. Several times in recent years, his
mother had tried to raise the issue of where she'd live
when he brought home a wife and started a family of
his own. Other times she'd suggested he might build
his own home. She'd picked out a hill overlooking the
highway and near the barns and told him he could
build there.

He hadn't listened. He'd never listened when she
talked about his future family. He'd always imagined
himself having too much fun to settle down, and since
a family was a long way off, why worry about it now?

Today had been a reality check. From his place on
the porch, he could hear the laughter inside: squeals

of and giggles from his niece, Cassie, nearly three, and from her older brother and sister, Tyler and Alice; deep bursts from Jim or Kurt or his brother-in-law, Bob; high, bird-like twitters from the newest family member, Kurt's bride, Alexa; deeper, gentler laughter from Jim's wife, Meg, or his sister, Joan; and the gentle duet of Wiley Richards' chortle mixed with his mother's bell-toned peals. It occurred to him that he'd heard her laugh more during the family dinner today than she had in the past year—maybe two. He'd always thought of her as happy, but until today, he'd never realized how much she might be missing.

So what would happen if she wanted to bring home a new husband? Chris pursed his lips in a thoughtful frown.

Another sound interrupted his reverie, the one he'd been studiously ignoring though it was never far from his thoughts. Sarah Richards McGill sat in the easy chair beside the front window, and inches from his place on the porch. During the entire visit since church today, throughout their Sunday dinner and the family sing-along afterward, throughout the visiting and the evening sandwiches and dessert, even through the women's chat while the men helped Chris with evening chores, Sarah had steadfastly avoided the children. She had said all the right things about what lovely children Joan and Bob had and how Jim and Meg's baby was "just adorable," but she had stayed away and Chris, standing beside her, had felt her tense whenever one of the kids, especially the baby, was near.

Then minutes ago, Meg had said she needed to use the bathroom and had unceremoniously handed the baby to Sarah, saying, "Here, you take her for a minute." Sarah had paled with a fear so palpable, Chris had felt tempted to run to her rescue, but Meg, acting as though she didn't notice, had dropped the baby into her lap anyway, and left the room.

Now Sarah sat in the easy chair with nine-month-old Alexis in her lap, playing peekaboo as naturally as if she did it every day. It was their laughter that intrigued Chris the most, the baby's shrill peals of giggles over the deep, rippling current of Sarah's laugh. The sound reached inside him, tightening his stomach, heightening his purely male interest, and creating an odd, tugging sensation in the vicinity of his heart.

Was it possible he was going to need a home for a family of his own? He'd never considered it before today, before Sarah. He took a deep breath and shook himself. Well, he couldn't consider it now, either. The lady had made it plain that she wasn't interested, that she wasn't going to be interested, hadn't she? Still, there was more to Sarah McGill than she was letting on. As he watched through the window, listening to the warm laughter from the woman and child inside, he promised himself he would discover all he could learn about the fascinating redhead who had swept into his life like a winter gale. After that, he'd follow wherever the trail led him. In the meantime, he was going to have to look into building a house on that hill.

*   *   *

Sarah stood at the top of the stairs, peeking out over the warm family scene in the McAllister parlor below her, her mind a whirlwind of thoughts and emotions. The day had been a tangle of interweaving threads— discoveries about herself, her thoughts and attitudes, her father . . . As she thought of him, she heard him laughing again, with Kate McAllister's corresponding laughter in the background. She couldn't remember when she'd ever heard her father sound this happy.

She had always thought of him as happy, fulfilled, satisfied. He had seemed so content in his work that she had copied his life in her own, carefully mirroring his education and his veterinary practice when her own life had been the most empty. But he hadn't been happy—not really, not ever during those long years alone.

And I've been planning to live alone. I thought it was the way to be happy. The thought hit Sarah like a stone. Was it possible that she needed to rethink her plans, her dreams? She'd heard of the concept of a paradigm shift. It was the kind of phenomenon that occurred when Copernicus proved the planets revolved around the sun, or Columbus demonstrated the earth was round. The world's scientists, caught in a false reality, had needed to shift their whole patterns of thinking in order to adapt. Was it possible she too needed a paradigm shift? A new way of perceiving her own world?

Meg's baby, Alexis, giggled and a jolt of mixed revulsion and pleasure ran through Sarah. For years she had made it a point to stay away from children.

Even when her roommate and best friend had started a day-care center, Sarah had stayed away, never visiting Eden at the center, seldom calling her there. By unspoken agreement, they had always talked about Eden's business practices and her management responsibilities, but they never discussed the kids. Eden understood Sarah, and helped her keep children at a distance.

Then an hour ago Meg had handed her baby to Sarah. Even when she'd protested, Meg had promised she'd only be gone a few minutes and had given her the baby anyway. She remembered clearly the anxiety she had felt as Meg dropped Alexis into her lap, and how her fear had slowly melted into pleasure at the infant's trusting smile. It had been pure joy to hold Alexis in her arms, to play with her and watch the light in her eyes as she caught on to the game and began to giggle. They had communicated in a way Sarah had never thought possible with a nine-month-old. It occurred to her then that she'd been so busy avoiding babies that she'd never had time to notice they were people—intelligent human beings with thoughts and ideas of their own. In those few moments while she had played with Alexis, years of her own fear and sorrow had melted away, evaporating like dew in sunshine.

Alexa, for whom the baby was named, said something the assembly downstairs found funny, and a ripple of laughter ran through the room. It tugged at Sarah's thoughts, helping her single out another emotion from the tangle she'd discovered today: yearning.

She hadn't known how much she'd missed this kind of family closeness, how much she'd wanted it. She hadn't even known that real people experienced this belonging until she'd seen it here today. She immediately felt cheated, wondering why she hadn't been allowed this pleasure. Then, when the moment of self-pity passed, her next emotion had been wonder. Might she, if she reorganized her goals, still find this warmth and joy?

She'd been pondering the discovery that babies were people when Meg had returned to claim her child and then, for no particular reason, had started talking about her own experience in coming back to Rainbow Rock and finding Jim again after ten years away. As if Sarah had asked for her life's story, Meg had recited the tale of her fears about commitment. She had told how, after watching her mother marry and divorce four times, she had been certain she had no talent for personal relationships, either. Then she told about Jim's tenderness and how he had simply loved her out of her insecurities, making her want a home and family, making her believe herself both worthy and capable of having them.

Entranced, Sarah had asked, "If you were so afraid of commitment, how did you ever allow Jim to get that close?"

"It was easy. He was my friend," Meg had answered with a meaningful glance at Chris, and Sarah's heart had swollen within her. She had immediately excused herself and gone upstairs, ostensibly to visit the rest room, but really needing to think.

What am I doing here? she thought as she watched the McAllisters below. *What will happen if I let Chris in, even as my friend?* She saw Meg and Jim smiling meaningfully at each other and wondered, *Is that what I want?* As she pondered, Chris stumbled into her line of vision, hot on the trail of young Tyler, his sister Joan's son. He caught the boy in a flying tackle and went down on his shoulder, carefully rolling to protect the child, then easing him to the floor and tickling until he screamed with delight.

She watched them, man and boy, and thought of how kind Chris had always been to her, even in the barn when she had deliberately insulted him. He was her friend—not just because he called himself that, but because he came through for her the way a friend would, trusted her as a friend would. *Trust.* She thought again of the knowing light in the baby's eyes when she had played with Alexis, then of the sympathetic way Chris had listened while she told him about her married life. Until she'd met Chris McAllister, she had found that kind of trust only with Eden and her mother.

He's a good man, a kind man, she thought, then she laughed aloud as she saw him take a fake karate kick from the self-professed superhero on the floor and collapse like a vanquished villain. *He'll make a great father.* She gasped. She couldn't guess where that last thought had come from, but it weakened her knees and left her breathless. Sarah moaned as she sat heavily on the steps and mumbled aloud, ''Oh, what am I doing here?''

*   *   *

"We're almost there," Chris said, smiling reassurance at Sarah, who sat as far away from him as the bench seat in his pickup would allow. If he'd been asked to characterize her expression, he'd have said she looked scared.

Chris swallowed a sigh. It had been almost two weeks since their Sunday dinner at his home and she had been an enigma ever since. Sometimes cool and distant, sometimes warm and encouraging, she seemed frustrated and confused at other times, and always a mystery to him.

That didn't keep him from being fascinated. Maybe it was even part of the fascination. The women he'd dated before had seemed girlish and predictable, or as shallow as lawn puddles. Sarah was like a sparkling jewel, constantly displaying new facets of her personality, each more lovely than the last.

"We're here," he said, pulling up near a hogan and setting the brake.

Sarah studied the beauty around her, the rich red earth spreading out in every direction, the red sandstone bluffs towering behind them, the grouping of small, earthen buildings that blended into the natural landscape. Already instructed in visitors' etiquette, she waited for the hogan's inhabitants to acknowledge their presence before opening her door. She was nervous about this trip, not just because she was going deep into the heart of *Dinehtah*, the precious Navajoland, but because it was becoming steadily more difficult to keep Chris at bay, or to remember why she wanted to.

A Navajo man in jeans and plaid flannel stepped into the dooryard and waved. Chris nodded to Sarah. They both opened their doors and walked toward the traditional eight-sided home. Chris greeted the man in Navajo, then haltingly explained his purpose. Sarah had heard the stories of how the McAllister children grew up speaking Navajo, having learned it from the woman who helped Kate in the house. Still, it impressed her to see how well Chris managed in a language that sounded utterly unintelligible to her English-trained ear.

Hosteen Begay, who had already been briefed by Logan, welcomed them warmly and led them around the hogan, corrals, and outbuildings to his corncrib. He spoke briefly to Chris, then left them to examine the crop on their own.

"This is his winter hogan," Chris explained as Begay left them. "They grow the corn in wide fields at their summer place. It's on a wash that runs in the spring and early summer. In the late summer, they depend on the afternoon rains. He says they will plant twice as much land this year, and turn the surplus crop over to the Greasewood project."

Sarah lifted a dried ear, still on the cob, and rubbed the kernels with ungloved fingers. "It still has some moisture in it, but not enough to spoil," she observed. "It looks like quality pig food."

"It's the same corn Begay grows to feed his family

through the winter," Chris answered. "The quality is excellent."

"From everything I can see, this project looks like a go.' " Sarah picked up another ear. "The Navajos have always raised corn. It seems odd that they're only now finding a way to capitalize."

"Maybe they haven't wanted to." Chris picked up an ear and began carefully removing a few kernels, showing her their size and thickness as he did. "The People don't value money the way our culture does, and their association with the corn plant is mostly sacred."

"Sacred?" Sarah asked.

"Um-hm. They believe they were formed of the corn."

"Really? I'd never heard that."

"According to legend, the earliest ancestors of the Dineh climbed up through the earth to emerge into another world, then another, then another. When they emerged into the Fourth World, they found it populated by the Kisani—that's the Navajo name for the Pueblo people of the Four Corners area. The Kisani were already here when the Navajo arrived, but they weren't the people of today, and the Navajos weren't, either."

"I don't understand."

"It takes some getting used to," Chris agreed, "but the Dineh believe their ancestors were other forms of life, animal-like beings with claws and fur."

"Sounds rather Darwinian to me." Sarah put a ker-

nel in her mouth, softening it with her teeth and
tongue.

"Maybe," Chris answered, "but it doesn't sound
that way when a medicine man tells it."

Sarah chuckled. "I'll take your word for that."

"Anyway," Chris continued, "the *yei*, the holy
people, came to visit the people of the Fourth World.
The ones that came were White Body, Blue Body,
Yellow Body, and Black Body. They talked to the
people and made signs and gestures, but the people
didn't understand what they were saying. They told
the people to bathe and cleanse themselves, then said
they'd return in twelve days to teach them more and
to make a new people, formed like themselves."

"Sounds like the Book of Genesis," Sarah inter-
jected, and the animation in her lovely features caused
a tender tug in the center of Chris's chest. "Did they
come in twelve days?"

"They did. That morning the People carefully
cleansed and purified themselves. Then the women
dried their bodies with yellow corn meal and the men
with white—"

"Why the difference?" Sarah asked, taking another
kernel.

"In Navajo mythology, yellow corn is only for female rites and white corn is for males. Ceremonies
always honor that difference. The story tells you
why."

"Okay." Sarah sat on a log near the corncrib.

"When the gods came, it was like the first time,
with the gods calling to the people before they arrived,

then after the fourth shout, they were there. Black Body and Blue Body each had a sacred buckskin, then White Body arrived with two perfect corn ears, one white and one yellow.'' He paused and handed her a particularly fat kernel from the ear he held. She popped it into her mouth. ''Then the gods took one of the two sacred buckskins and laid it on the earth with its head toward the west. They took the two ears of corn and laid them upon the buckskin with their tips toward the east—''

''Why are the directions important?''

''The four cardinal directions are highly sacred to Navajo thinking. Different things come from different directions, and it's important to know what comes from where. I'd explain more, but it's complicated, and . . .'' He paused meaningfully. ''I seem to be having trouble getting through this story as it is.''

Sarah sparkled at him, her eyes alight. ''Okay, okay. I can take a hint,'' she grumbled in mock anger.

He smiled. ''So they laid the corn on the sacred buckskin—''

''—tips to the east—''

''—tips to the east,'' he acknowledged, ''and under each they put an eagle feather, a white eagle feather for the white corn and a yellow eagle feather for the yellow corn. When that was done, they took the second sacred buckskin and spread it over the corn ears with its head to the east. Then they told the people to stand back and allow the wind to blow.''

''I'll bet it blew,'' Sarah volunteered.

''Of course it did.'' Chris dropped down beside

Sarah, squatting on his haunches. "While it was blowing, the Mirage People—more holy folks—came and walked around the skins four times. As they did, the tips of the eagle feathers began to move. When the Mirage People finished their walk and the buckskin was pulled back, the ears of corn were gone. The yellow corn had become a human woman and the white corn a man. They were the First Man and First Woman of the Navajo people, something like our Adam and Eve."

"Ah, now I see why the colors are important," Sarah said. "The People believe they are made of corn?"

"Corn and wind," Chris clarified. "They say it is the wind that gives us breath. When our breath stops, we die."

"That makes sense," Sarah acknowledged. A haunting quiet settled over them as they sat near Begay's corncrib, and for a moment, Sarah almost believed she could sense the presence of the Navajo ancestors. In this primeval setting, she and Chris could almost have been the First Man and First Woman of their own people. She shook her head. Seldom one to engage in flights of fancy, she'd found them all too easy to indulge in lately—since returning to Rainbow Rock, since meeting Chris McAllister. She rose from the log, lifting the ear she held. "This is good, sweet corn. It'll be great for fattening pigs."

"My thoughts exactly." They started back toward the truck.

But Sarah had not fully shaken the spirit of the ancients. "That story you just told me, about human creation—do the Navajo people still believe these myths?"

"Almost to a person," Chris answered, "at least here on the reservation. Many of those who choose to leave no longer hold the traditions sacred, but among those who stay, the legends are as much scripture as the Bible is to you or me."

"Do the Navajos have an organized religion, then? I mean, with churches and priests and such?"

"Yes and no. There are no churches, no priests, no holy objects—at least, not in the sense that most Anglos think of them. In fact, when Europeans first encountered the Navajo, they told other Anglos that the People had no religion, because they didn't see any evidence of it. What they didn't recognize is the Dineh don't separate their faith from the rest of their life as many Anglos do. They don't have churches, but their homes and fields are holy places. They don't have priests as such, partly because every Navajo is expected to worship, and to perform sacred ceremonies, although they do have singers and other holy men, whose training helps them lead special ceremonies. They don't have many holy objects, either, because they consider everything around them holy."

"Like the corn they plant," Sarah said, touching the ear she still carried.

"Exactly," Chris answered.

They arrived at the hogan and Chris spoke again to Hosteen Begay, explaining in Navajo that the corn was good and he should plan to plant a large crop. Then they said their good-byes and got into the truck.

"What about the educated Navajos?" Sarah asked as they drove away. "The people like Logan."

"Do you mean do they believe in the ancient legends?"

"Right."

"It's their faith. It doesn't go away just because they go to school." Chris slowed to ease his way through a washout in the road. "For several generations the Dineh have sent their children to the white man's schools to 'learn paper.' When they finish school, they usually return to the traditions of their ancestors or come back in a different capacity, the way Logan did."

"About Logan," Sarah said, not sure how to proceed. She knew Chris felt close to the man he called the Copper Crusader, and she didn't want to offend him. At the same time, she did want to clear the air. "Sometimes I feel a real tension around him," she said. "Almost hostility. Am I imagining it? Or does Logan not like me much?"

Chris smiled with a look like an apology and Sarah breathed relief. At least she hadn't offended Chris by asking. "I don't think you're imagining it."

"So he doesn't like me?"

"Probably not, but don't take it personally."

Sarah's brow lifted in a question. "How am I *supposed* to take it?"

"Logan is distrustful of *belagaana*, especially *belagaana* women."

"*Belagaana*? That means white?"

"Technically it means 'other,' not Navajo. But in practice it usually refers to Anglos."

"So why does he want me on the project if he doesn't trust me?"

"Because he knows you're good." Chris paused. "And because I recommended you."

"Oh." Sarah took a moment to digest that. "You're *belagaana*. How'd you get in good with him?"

"We were roommates at ASU, assigned to each other by the dormitories. He really had a big chip on his shoulder in those days—"

"Worse than now?"

"Much worse, and he told me on the first night that he hated me."

Sarah felt queasy. "That sounds like the start of a beautiful friendship."

Chris shrugged. "Crazy, maybe, but it was. He stood there with his fists clenched, telling me how he hated white people, and I knew I had to do something. So I punched him."

"You *what*?" Sarah gaped, wide-eyed.

"I punched him," Chris repeated. "Knocked the wind out of him and put him on the floor. He wasn't hurt, just humiliated. Then while he was still too stunned to get up, I sat on his chest and held him down. I started speaking in Navajo, very quietly, telling him that I knew him, that I knew his people and his clan. I told him I thought the Navajo were the Dineh, The People, chosen of the holy ones, that I valued Dinehtah as a holy place and loved its language and its art. He just lay there, staring at me in shock. When I got up, I offered him my hand and he took it."

"And that was the end of it?"

"Hardly. The next day he walked into the room after classes and found me there, looking out the window with my back to him. He called me by name, and when I turned around, he punched me hard, right in the stomach. He knocked me to the floor. Then he laughed. As soon as I could get my breath, I laughed too. Then he offered me his hand and helped me up. From that time on, we've been the best of friends."

Sarah shook her head. "Hard as I may try, I'll never understand men. If a couple of women punched each other out like that, they'd never speak to each other again."

He shrugged. "I guess it's a guy thing."

"I guess so." She paused. "Chris? What happened to Logan to make him so bitter?"

"Mostly, the same things that happened to other Navajos." He paused. "The relationship between their people and our government has never been much to brag about."

"I know." Sarah had heard the tales of hardship and abuse, of Indian slavery, of treaties made and broken, all at the expense of the Navajo. "But there's something else going on. With Logan, it's personal."

"Yeah, it is," Chris said. He looked uncomfortable. "Look, everything I know, Logan told me in confidence. If I share it with you, you'll need to treat it the same way."

Sarah nodded. "I understand."

"His mother was *belagaana*."

"What? A white woman?"

"Yeah. Marianne Logan, a flower child from the wealthier districts of San Francisco who spent her summers singing about free love in Haight Ashbury. Somewhere along the way, a group of her friends decided they were going to 'go native,' so they loaded up a hippie bus and drove to the reservation. Nobody knows exactly how they landed in Greasewood, but Marianne struck up a friendship with Albert Redhorse that quickly turned into a love affair. By the time her friends decided to split and go home, she was calling herself Morning Light, braiding her hair, and living in a hogan Albert had built for her. They were married in a traditional ceremony, no legal documents, a few days later."

"Morning Light? That doesn't sound like a Navajo name."

"It isn't. And Navajo women don't braid their hair. The men don't either, for that matter. But authenticity wasn't as important to Marianne as the dream. That lasted just long enough for her to give birth in a hogan, without a doctor or modern medicine. By then, she was little more than a ghost of the girl who had come to the rez. Nothing had been as she expected. Albert wanted her to be happy, but he couldn't offer what he didn't have. Marianne had grown steadily paler and more depressed all through the pregnancy, then when she went through a long, difficult labor with no one but Albert's mother to help her, it was more than she could take. When the baby, still unnamed, was just a few days old, she left him in a basket, hitched a ride into Holbrook, and called her parents for a bus ticket. They shipped her home immediately. End of story.''

Sarah tried to swallow down the lump in her throat. ''That was all? She never came back? Never wanted to see her son?''

''Never,'' Chris answered. ''A few months later, her parents sent Albert some paperwork. They'd established a college fund for the child Marianne had left, and they made it clear that the money was intended to discharge any obligation they may have had. Seems they didn't want a half-Indian kid to clutter up their lives on Snob Hill.''

Sarah hissed through her teeth. ''No wonder Logan is bitter.''

''In a way, it gets worse.''

''Worse?''

''The Navajo people are matrilineal. Family, clan ties, property, even one's place in the tribe are all inherited through the mother. Albert Redhorse kept his son, and his mother, Logan's grandmother, raised him almost as if he were her own, but—''

''—but without a Navajo mother, Logan had no place among his people,'' Sarah finished, making the logical connection.

''Right,'' Chris answered. ''His grandmother's clan has always claimed him, but everyone knows his mother is *belagaana*, and that she abandoned him. Whether his people treat him that way or not, Logan feels a stigma, like he isn't really one of them, like he doesn't belong.''

''No wonder he's bitter,'' Sarah said again, suddenly feeling much greater sympathy for the man she had come to see as cold and distant.

''He won't be happy with me if he knows I told you,'' Chris finished.

''I won't say anything,'' Sarah promised. They traveled in silence, each cloaked in thought, both moved by the retelling of Logan's disinheritance. Chris was feeling that same kind of distance from Sarah and wondering how he could break through the barriers he often found, erected like palisades around Sarah's heart. Sarah was thinking she might never again meet a man like Chris, a man with his warmth and understanding. Maybe she could risk coming to know him better, risk caring about him more.

Darkness fell over Rainbow Rock as they pulled up beside the veterinary truck in the driveway at her father's home. Chris came around to open Sarah's door, expecting to help her down. That worked just as he expected, but when her feet touched the pavement, she whispered, ''Don't go yet,'' and put her arms around his neck.

Chris felt his heart rate increase. Did that look in her eyes really mean she intended to kiss him? What did this thaw in the weather mean?

''Thank you for taking me with you today,'' she whispered, rising up on her tiptoes. ''Thank you for telling me about the corn, and about Logan.''

''I trust you,'' he answered simply.

"Thank you for that, too." She looked directly into his eyes and brought her lips closer, then pulled his head toward hers.

Chris eagerly complied, turning his head and taking her mouth in a tender kiss. It was Sarah's idea to deepen that kiss, Sarah who leaned into the embrace. When Chris feared he had had enough of heaven and tried to pull away, it was Sarah who drew him close again, leaving his senses churning and his mind reeling with the power that passed between them.

When she finally let him go, Chris felt unsteady on his feet. "Remind me to do nice things for you often," he murmured. "If you're going to thank me like that . . ." He smiled, leaving the sentence hanging.

"How about tomorrow?" Sarah asked, her eyes shining.

"Tomorrow . . . what?"

"Want to invite me to the family dinner again?" She walked toward her front door, looking coquettishly over her shoulder.

"I thought—" Chris cut off the idea. "Sure, you're always welcome. In fact, I think your dad is already planning to come. You can come with him."

She stopped at the doorway. "I'd rather come with you." The invitation in her eyes was clear.

"I'll pick you up tomorrow morning," he answered, opening the door.

"For church, too?"

"For church, too. Let's make it nine o'clock."

She beamed a sunny smile and Chris could have sworn that, for a moment, the earth turned backward and the sun peeked over the horizon. ''I'll see you then,'' she whispered, and touched her lips to his again.

Chris stood rooted to the porch while she entered the house and closed the door behind her, then he walked slowly back to the truck and started for home, wondering all the way what had changed—and whether he could maintain this sudden warm front.

Sarah stood at the living room window, watching as Chris drove away. She'd confused him; she knew she had. That didn't bother her, so long as he liked the difference. She sighed, hoping she was doing the right thing.

Chapter Six

Chris never knew what had caused the thaw, but it continued through the end of February and all of March as well. At first, he wasn't quite sure where he stood, or how to proceed. Then Sarah started making excuses to drop by the farm when she didn't have to. A few days later, she invited him to see a movie with her. Flummoxed, he asked, "You mean, like a date?"

She had given him that coquettish look again, mischief dancing in her turquoise eyes, and answered, "Can't a friend invite a friend to the movies?"

He'd been more than happy to agree, but Sarah had confused him even more by the way she'd behaved later in the theater—taking his hand, holding his arm, acting much more like a date than a pal. And she had continued to act that way.

She became a regular guest at Sunday family dinners—she and Wiley both—and started asking Kate what dishes she could bring to help out the next week. She went with Chris every Saturday to examine progress on the Greasewood hog farm, and invited him for an occasional dinner at her place. She stopped by often, sometimes without an excuse, and when he tentatively began to suggest activities he thought she'd enjoy, she eagerly accepted. By mid-March, all of Rainbow Rock and most of Holbrook knew Chris and Sarah were dating.

In early March they took a day off. Chris pressed his brothers into service on the farm and Sarah refused to schedule appointments, so they could visit the Anasazi ruins at Wupatki. Wandering among the remnants of the village where ancient generations had lived and loved, worked and worried, cared and carried on, they had looked more like lovers than friends, and Chris found he was thinking and feeling more like a lover as well.

On the twenty-fourth of March they drove to Joseph City to watch the Founder's Day parade trek down a half mile of Main Street with the combined marching band from the junior and senior high schools in the lead. Then they joined the community for barbecue, beans, and cole slaw in the bus barn by the old school gym.

They were driving back toward Holbrook when Sarah picked up a magazine she'd purchased in town that morning. The cover showed a field full of daffodils. ''I couldn't resist,'' she said as she showed Chris the cover photo. ''Daffodils have always been my favorites.''

''You don't see many in our neck of the woods,'' he answered.

''No, this isn't great country for growing bulbs.'' Sarah set the magazine on the floor. ''My mother used to have daffodils in the planter by our back porch,'' she said, her eyes dreamy, focused on the past. ''I planted some there when I was in high school, but they're long since gone.'' She sat quietly for a moment, then turned to Chris again and said, ''Well, enough of memories. Maybe I'll buy some potted ones this spring. If I put them out this fall, they can bloom in Dad's planter next year.''

Chris put his hand on her knee. In recent weeks, she had started buckling in to the center seat belt instead of the far one. He heartily approved the change. ''I can see you in daffodils,'' he said, smiling warmly. ''You always look gorgeous in yellow.''

She answered with a surprised smile. ''Thank you, Chris. That was very kind.''

''Not kind. True.''

She put her hand over his. ''Maybe that's part of the reason I like them. They flatter my red hair. Maybe that's why I like amethysts, too.''

''Amethysts?'' Chris turned in surprise.

''You know, purple gemstones. Amethysts.''

''I don't think I've ever seen you wear jewelry.''

''I don't wear it often,'' she agreed. ''Too risky when I'm working around animals and farms. An earring could get caught in baling wire and ripped out of my ear. A cow could try to swallow a necklace and end up eating much of my neck instead.''

''I hadn't thought of it that way,'' Chris answered.

Sarah was quiet for a moment before she said, ''But I do like amethysts, even if I don't wear them often.''

''I'm sure you'd look lovely in amethysts, too,'' Chris said, touching her gently, then he made a mental note to remember both the flowers and the gemstones.

Through the first week of April they spent every evening together, usually at his home or hers, though they sometimes went into town. Chris had stopped wondering about the quality of their relationship, and had begun thinking instead about its future. He wasn't sure whether he was ready for long-term commitments, but he knew he cared about Sarah in ways he had never cared for another woman, and he enjoyed being with her more than with anyone he knew. He made an appointment for the middle of April to have a builder friend come out to look at his hill.

Then something happened. It was a Friday evening and they had planned to drive into Holbrook. Chris hurried through his evening chores so he could arrive early at Sarah's, then he had to pull around the now-familiar obstacle of Wiley's little compact in order to get out of the driveway. Then when he got to the Richards home, he found it dark, apparently deserted.

He combed his hair back with his fingers and grimaced in frustration, wondering, *What now?* It was too cold for waiting on the porch. Storm clouds threatened in the eastern sky and the chill in the air felt like snow.

Vaguely disquieted, he climbed back into the cab of his pickup truck, turned on the heater, and waited. And waited. After half an hour, he was nervous. When nearly an hour had passed, he was verging on panic. He had almost decided to start calling police agencies and hospitals when the veterinary truck drove up beside him. Not even acknowledging his presence, Sarah got out on the driver's side, then hurried to help Wiley.

Chris ran to help. "What's wrong? What's happened?" he asked, taking Wiley's arm.

Sarah all but pushed him out of the way, sliding under her father's shoulder and putting her arm around him. "I can't talk to you now," she said, not even looking his way. "I need to get Dad inside."

"But why? What happened?" He had thought Wiley was doing so well lately, out of the cast now and walking with a cane.

Sarah threw him a look designed to melt glass. "Why don't you ask your mother?" she hissed.

Chris watched in stunned silence as father and daughter hobbled inside the front door, letting it slam behind them. "My mother?" he mumbled aloud. Minutes later, he arrived in the family dooryard, pulling in beside Wiley's compact.

"Mom?" he called as he entered the parlor. She didn't answer, but he could hear odd little hiccuping sounds coming from the kitchen. "Mom?" he asked again, more quietly, as he arrived in the kitchen doorway to find Kate sitting at the table, her head on her arms, quietly crying her heart out. He sat next to her, carefully touching her shoulder. "Mom? What's wrong?"

She looked up, eyes red and swollen, and burbled, "No-thing."

The irony and the release of tension were almost more than Chris could stand. He had to bite his lip to keep from laughing. "Um, Mom, I know something's wrong. Wiley is hurt, Sarah won't talk to me, and you don't usually cry at the kitchen table."

Kate raised her head. "Sarah?" She sniffed. "Sarah won't talk to you?"

Encouraged, Chris pressed on. "When I asked what was wrong with Wiley, she said, 'Ask your mother.' "

"Oh, dear." Kate drew a long, shaky breath, trying to compose herself. "Oh, dear," she said again. "I didn't think it would ever—" She interrupted herself with another fit of tears.

Over the next several minutes, Chris managed to coax out much of the story. Though his mother still refused to share details, he was able to gather that Kate and Wiley had argued and Wiley had left in a huff. Then somehow he had fallen, landing on his injured knee. When he had been unable to get up by himself, Kate had called the number for the veterinary office and Sarah, running late after putting down a prize Jersey cow that had apparently swallowed barbed wire, had taken the call on her cellular phone. From that point on, Chris could pretty much deduce the rest.

"Are you going to be okay?" he asked his mother, as he handed her yet another tissue.

"Yes. I'm ... just fine," she burbled, doing her best to pretend.

"Then I think maybe I'll go back to the Richards place to see if I can make peace there." He stood. "Would you like to come?"

Kate looked horrified. "No! Oh, no, I c-couldn't!"

He took her hand, then asked her gently, "Are you sure?"

She sniffed again. "Oh, yes, quite sure."

"All right, then." Chris picked up his coat. He managed a wry smile. "This could take a while."

Kate nodded. "I won't wait up."

All the way to the Richards home, Chris worried. Whatever had happened between their parents, he felt certain it should remain between them and not be visited on the next generation. The problem, as he saw it, was persuading Sarah of that. He practiced approaches as he drove, but still felt unprepared by the time he knocked on the door, then knocked again. He had almost worn the skin off his knuckles by the time she answered, and even then she kept the chain lock on, barely wedging the door open. "What do you want?" she asked, her voice rife with suspicion.

"I've come to see you, Sarah." Chris adopted his most reasonable tone. "We were supposed to have dinner, remember?"

She answered archly. "In view of what's happened ..."

"Nothing has happened between us," he corrected. "If our parents are having problems, I think that's their business.'' He reached through the door, hoping to touch her hand.

''Go away!'' she said, and almost slammed his hand in the door.

Luckily, he had placed his foot as a doorstop, though the attempted slam caused some bruises he knew he'd feel later. ''Let me in,'' he said gently. ''We need to talk.''

''I don't *want* to talk to you!''

Chris could see about half of Sarah's face. He wondered if the anger he saw there should have thrilled him as much as it did. ''Sarah, you're not being fair,'' he said, trying again. ''I didn't do anything to your father. And if my mother did, well, maybe she had a good reason—or thought she did.''

''How dare you?''

If anger looked good on Sarah, rage was positively magnificent. Chris wanted to sweep her up and kiss the storm clouds away. ''You do have to consider the possibility that it wasn't all my mother's fault,'' he said, pressing her, ''and that it wasn't my fault at all.''

''I don't want to—'' Sarah began, but her father interrupted.

Stepping into the front room, Wiley said, ''He's right, honey. Talk to the boy.''

''Dad! You should be resting.''

Through the crack in the door, Chris could see Wiley Richards limping into the room, resting heavily on his cane. ''I'm fine, honey,'' he assured his daughter. ''And I'm going to *be* fine. The boy's right. Kate and

I will have to manage our own problems. Now go on to dinner and have a good time.''

"But Dad!" Sarah sounded like a whiny teenager. Chris found it rather cute.

"Go on, now. Talk to him," Wiley said from inside.

Her eyes still smoldering—that is, her right eye, the one Chris could see—Sarah turned to look at Chris again. "If you'll let me close the door, I can take the chain lock off."

"Sure thing," he answered amiably, withdrawing his foot and letting the door swing closed. It seemed to take a long time before it opened again, and Sarah, not at all mollified, stepped out.

"I really don't want to go out tonight," she began, wrapping her arms about herself in a gesture that looked more like protection from him than from the cold. "In spite of what Dad says, I'm very upset. I don't think I'd make good company."

"Okay, so we won't go out," Chris said gently, though he found his patience wearing thin. "Maybe we can just sit and talk a minute."

"It's cold," Sarah answered, looking for all the world like a petulant child.

"I've noticed." Chris turned up the lamb's-wool collar of his denim jacket to cover his neck and ears. "Maybe you could invite me in?"

Sarah flashed an angry look at him, then toward the house. "We can talk in your truck," she said.

Chris felt his patience ebbing. "Look, Sarah—"

"Don't start! Don't you dare start! You don't know

what I've been through tonight!'' She put a hand
against his chest as if to hold him back, but just about
then the tears started.

Chris didn't know how it happened, but in one moment he was considering how he might protect himself
if faced with a screaming banshee. In the next, he was
holding a sobbing, half-hysterical woman who clung
to him as if he was the last bastion of safety left on
earth.

"Oh, Chris!" she sobbed against his chest. "Hold
me! Hold me, please!"

"Sure, honey," he crooned gently, cuddling her
close. "Shh, shh, it's all right now. Everything's all
right."

During the next hour, in a pattern that was beginning to seem all too familiar, Chris coaxed a second
sobbing woman into telling him her story. After the
first few minutes, they migrated into the warmth of the
living room. Minutes later, they barely noticed as Wiley grabbed his coat and hat and left by the front door.
By the end of the hour, hysteria and clinging had
turned into snuggling and tender touches. Though
Chris still wasn't sure what had happened, he was
grateful it had.

"Then it was really your memories that had you the
most upset," he said as she finished her tale.

"I guess so," Sarah answered, finally able to silence the tears. "I told you Jake wasn't rough with
me, and he wasn't—usually. But there was that one
time, and it was bad."

Chris gritted his teeth, barely able to stand his mental pictures of the scene Sarah had just described.

"When it was over, he was all apologies, but I was all bruises. And that was the last time I saw him before that last weekend. I think that was why we argued so much that last couple of days before . . . before Cheyenne."

Chris released a deep breath. "So when you saw our parents arguing and knew your dad was hurt, you thought—"

"I didn't think at all. I just went ballistic. All I could picture was my dad and your mom shrieking at each other the way Jake and I used to. I'd had a bad day anyway, and then, when I saw Dad hurt . . ." The words trailed off in a shudder.

Chris pulled her tighter against him. "What I don't understand is why you were mad at me. I wasn't even there when they argued."

She shook her head. "I know you weren't, and I'm not sure why I got so angry. More distancing, maybe. I panicked. That's all I can say. I just panicked. You and I . . . well, we've been getting closer lately, and, well . . ."

"You were afraid that if I made any claims, I might hurt you the way Jake did, the way you thought my mom was hurting your dad."

She drew a deep, shaky breath. "Maybe. I'm not sure. I don't think I was thinking much at the time."

"But everything's okay now." He held her at arm's length and peered into her eyes, amusement lighting his features. "Isn't it?"

She nodded, smiling through the last stubborn tears. "Yes, I think so." She touched his face. "Thanks for being so patient, Chris. Thanks for not letting me drive you away, even when I was trying my hardest."

"Well, there was a minute there . . ." Chris said, but his grin told her he was joking, and she poked him playfully as she laughed and called him a tease. Then, for a long while, they just held each other, laughing and cuddling and kissing now and then.

It was late when Chris finally noticed the time. "You know," he said, "one thing we still haven't done tonight is dinner."

"That must mean you're hungry."

"Starving!"

"Then come with me to the kitchen. I think between the two of us, we can round up something."

"Let's go!" he answered, pulling her off the couch.

Working together, they scrambled eggs and made toast, started coffee, and popped a couples of potatoes into the microwave. Within a few minutes they were seated at the table, enjoying the simple meal like an old, long-married couple. Chris liked the sensation. He liked it a lot. He wondered if Sarah liked it, too.

"Sarah?" he asked as he set his plate in the sink.

"Hmm?" she answered.

Then the front door swung opened and they heard Wiley enter. "Anybody home?" he called.

Sarah looked to Chris.

"Later," he whispered, slow to release her hand.

She smiled, then turned toward the front room. "In here, Dad." Wiley joined them a moment later. Kate

was with him. Sarah looked from one to the other in
open surprise. "Looks like you've mended your dif-
ferences."

"We thought you might both be here," Kate said.
"We wanted you to be the first to know." Chris
looked at Sarah, then at his mother and Wiley. Shock
washed over him as he realized what Kate was about
to say. Then she said it. "We've decided to be married."

Wiley let out a rebel yell and swung Kate in a circle,
then moaned and grabbed his knee. Kate laughed and
called him a "beautiful old fool." Chris and Sarah just
sat looking at each other, their faces inscribed with
surprise.

Declaring they saw no point in waiting once they
had made up their minds, Kate and Wiley planned
their wedding for May Day on the front porch of the
McAllister home. They asked Sarah and Chris to stand
up with them, and the Reverend Phelps offered his
services as a gift to two longtime parishioners. Joan,
Meg, and Alexa nominated themselves a committee of
three to handle food for a simple reception afterward,
Bob coordinated the guest list, and Kurt asked Jim to
help him round up tables and chairs. The children, all
except baby Alexis, were enlisted to carry the flowers
and rings.

Without adequate time to print invitations, the couple bought small ads in local papers, inviting their
friends to join them, and everyone in the family, in-

cluding Sarah, had his or her own list of people to call for personal invitations.

One of the next questions was the matter of where Kate and Wiley would live. Wiley answered that quickly. Kate, he declared, was determined that Chris should stay on the farm. That meant they'd return from a brief honeymoon to live in the Richards home, and that gave Sarah less than a month to find a place and move her things.

Between the plans for the coming ceremony and the task of finding an apartment, Chris and Sarah stayed busy during April—and sadly distant. Though they were together for several hours every day, Chris missed the closeness they had achieved for those few brief moments on the night of their parents' decision. As he sat looking blankly at his portion of the guest list, he wondered if it was the stress of all the changes she was experiencing that kept Sarah so cool and polite, or if maybe she was bothered by the family taunts about how they'd soon be brother and sister, a claim he was quick to qualify.

From time to time as he watched her working and planning to move into her new efficiency apartment downtown, he remembered how close he had felt to her that evening, and how he had almost asked a fateful question, one that would make them think out loud about the future of their relationship. Now, with the freeze on again, he wasn't sure if he wanted to ask it—at least not before the spring thaw. He sat down at the kitchen table, the desk phone in front of him, and started working on his wedding list.

*   *   *

Sarah finished taping the box she had just packed and stood, hands on hips. Everything was finished except the bottom drawer in the built-in cupboard, and it wouldn't take long to pack that. Chris and his brothers would arrive early tomorrow, each in his own pickup, so by noon she'd be moved out of the room that had been her security since childhood.

"What's the matter with me, anyway?" she asked her room. "It isn't as if I haven't left before." She had hoped to persuade herself by saying it aloud, but the echo in the near-empty room only lowered her spirits. She had never taken *all* her things; maybe she was really leaving for the very first time.

She sighed and steeled herself to face the bottom drawer. Moving an empty box and a trash can near, she began the process of sorting through things she had left since her high school years. She found some letters from a pen pal in Switzerland, the last one more than twelve years old. She hadn't thought of Helga in years. The letters went into the can. Under them were the programs from several school dances—those she remembered fondly went into the box, others she didn't remember at all went into the can. There were a couple of grade cards, which she quickly threw away, and some photographs of her with her high school pals. She thumbed through them, smiling at the memories they triggered, then carefully put each into the box. Then she picked up the next photo, saw her mother, and gasped as her heart did a painful twist.

The snapshot had been taken in Sarah's earliest

childhood. The woman in it was vibrant and young, her long, dark hair streaming halfway to her waist, a lover's smile beaming at the man behind the camera. Sarah moaned and shut her eyes against the sorrow that threatened to swallow her.

Since her father and Kate had announced their engagement, Sarah had kept herself too busy to wonder how she felt. She knew that, despite her outward efforts to do and say all the right things, she hadn't been as happy for the couple as they might have hoped. Sometimes she had wondered if she didn't feel jealous of her dad's interest in Kate. Though she disliked that thought, she had to admit there was some basis for it. She'd had her dad—that is, what little she'd had of him—to herself all these years. It wasn't easy to see someone else taking the premier position in his life.

She remembered the night of the big argument and how furious she had been at Kate for hurting her father. She had gone to his defense in a rush, then felt spurned when he'd sided with Chris. Then, when her father had come home with Kate by his side, she had felt . . . She hunted for the right word. *Betrayed*, that was what she had felt—and now she knew it was not just for herself. She felt betrayed on behalf of the beautiful woman in the picture, Diane Richards, the one her father had promised to love forever. He'd been faithful to her mother for more than twenty years after she was gone. It hurt Sarah to see him leave her now.

Then with another flash of insight, she recognized that even that concern was really for herself. If Jake could leave her, and her mother could leave her father, and her father could leave her mother's memory, wasn't that proof that any love could end? That all love would end?

She sat flat on the floor and leaned against the bed, allowing that thought to percolate. So it was her own fear of commitment and loss that had led to her resentment. Was that fair to her father? To Kate? . . . to Chris?

''Oh, Chris!'' she said aloud, slumping against the bed with a sigh. She'd been so unfair to him these last weeks, so cool and distant . . . Distant. Here she was distancing again—and after her effort this spring when she had deliberately escalated their relationship. What must Chris be thinking?

She hurried to the phone in her father's hallway and quickly dialed Chris's number, ready to tell him all she had discovered, to ask him to forgive her yet again. The line was busy.

Disheartened, she went back to finish packing, but the internal inspection she had begun wasn't over yet. With chagrin she recalled scenes from the time she'd re-met Chris—the way she'd pegged him as a chauvinist the first time she saw him, then called him Goldilocks; the time she'd insulted him in the barn; her childishness on the night her father had called from Kate's house; her selfishness—that was all she could call it—since she had begun to pursue him.

Chris was a good man, a kind man. He deserved better than she had to give him. The rest of the papers she packed that night were stained with her tears.

Chapter Seven

Chris stood on the porch of the home that was now his, listening as his mother took her vows. Everything had gone perfectly for Kate and Wiley so far this morning, and there was every expectation that they would have a lovely wedding day and a great beginning to their life together.

On the other side of the bridal couple, Sarah shone in a fitted, butter-yellow dress, yellow rosebuds twisted into her soft French braid. Chris caught her gaze and smiled. She returned the smile with a sunny burst of warmth that beamed like the sun breaking through storm clouds and he felt a rush of tenderness that was utterly, marvelously new.

Is this love? he asked himself, almost sure he knew the answer. Sarah had come to feel like another part of him, a piece of his life. He already loved the way she looked at him when her temper was piqued and the way she said his name when attraction thickened her voice. He loved those marvelous turquoise eyes and the flash he could sometimes excite in them. He loved the commitment she felt to her father and her work and a childhood friend named Eden whom she adored with sisterly devotion. He loved that she could be cute and kittenish one moment, and as thoughtful and wise as a sage the next. Her loved her biting humor and her sometimes sarcastic wit, and the delicate whiteness of her skin. He loved . . .

He paused and looked at her as if he'd never seen her before. He loved Sarah. He loved her! The moment of realization was an epiphany like nothing he had ever experienced, and in that moment, Chris saw himself as a marrying man, a family man happy to get up in the night with babies, or change diapers, or clean up baby spit, or . . . He looked at his brothers, pride glowing in their faces as they held their families close, and he knew that was what he wanted, and that now he felt ready.

He gazed again at Sarah with a look of such intense anticipation that she turned with a quizzical expression on her face, almost as if she had heard the question he had not yet asked. He felt the muscle in his jaw tense as he looked at her, trying to tell her with his eyes everything he did not yet dare say. The spell hung over them for long, precious seconds while Chris basked in the delight of his discovery. Then the minister asked him for the ring and he reluctantly gave his attention to the matter at hand.

But he did not forget his Sarah, not for a moment. As the ceremony ended with the minister telling Wiley to kiss his bride, he took Sarah's hand. When the new-lyweds turned to greet the applause of their assembled family and friends, he drew her close against him. While friends and neighbors filed by in an informal receiving line, he kept her beside him, beaming sunny smiles at her whenever he could catch her eye. Maybe he hadn't yet had a chance to tell her how he felt—and maybe, now that he considered it, he wouldn't hurry that revelation until he felt sure she was ready to hear it—but he wanted her to start feeling it now. He wanted to warm her in the light of his love until she glowed with it, radiating it back to him. He wanted to love her so completely, so purely, that the power of it could bind her to him and keep her beside him forever.

As he stood in the company of family and friends, watching as Kate cut the cake her friend Lois had baked fresh yesterday, he promised himself he would woo Sarah, court her, romance her, until the last of the cold front had melted and the warmth beneath shone through. Then and only then would he ask her to marry him.

Wiley chuckled as Kate tried to feed him a glob of frosting in the shape of a yellow rose, and Chris caught Sarah's gaze again, his eyes promising forever.

*   *   *

Sarah folded the last of the tablecloths and stacked it with the others Joan had volunteered to wash. When she turned, Chris would probably be there. She didn't know what had come over him today, but the eerie intensity of his gaze, the dedication in the way he watched her, was at least as unnerving as it was flattering.

Minutes ago, her father had driven away with his new bride, the two of them in the front seat of his little town car on their way to Sky Harbor in Phoenix. There they planned to spend an undisturbed wedding night before catching a plane the next morning. Sarah had kissed her father's cheek, then Kate's, tearfully wishing them a happy life and sending them on their way, but her tears had been expressions of happiness and her wishes had been from her heart. As much as she still felt cheated and saddened by her mother's early death, she knew the time had long since come for her father and Kate to find some happiness.

What she didn't know was whether her father's daughter would ever know the same opportunity. She straightened her spine, steeling herself to turn around and face Chris again. He seemed so eager, so ardent, so *young*. The more she came to care about him, the more she knew he deserved better than the very best she could give.

"Looks like we're about finished here." Alexa stood just behind her right shoulder and Sarah turned gratefully, not yet ready to face both Chris and her own confusion.

"It was a lovely wedding, wasn't it?" she asked.

"Almost as lovely as my own," Alexa answered. "Did I ever tell you about it?"

"Why no, but—" Sarah began, but Alexa was already talking.

"I was sure I didn't want to get married, at least for a long time. I was on my way to Hollywood to interview for a job as a scriptwriter when my car went off the road and Kurt came to my rescue. Almost before I knew it, I was falling in love with him."

"But you still went to Hollywood," Sarah reminded. The family had briefed her on that part of the story.

"I went, but I couldn't stay," Alexa answered. "I thought I wanted independence, the chance to be on my own and at the top of my profession."

Sarah shivered, caught up in the story despite herself. She'd spent the last several years thinking the same thing.

"What I didn't realize was, being at the top of anything isn't much fun if you can't share it with people you care about." She was looking at Sarah with the same kind of scrutiny Chris had been giving her all day. "I knew then that what I really wanted was Kurt."

Sarah remembered the day Meg had told her story. She was beginning to suspect a family plot. "But you're still a screenwriter."

"True. I'm lucky enough to have the best of both worlds. In fact, we start filming this next project in about three weeks. Kurt's going to take some time off to fly out with me when I go to work on the set."

Sarah smiled. "That's wonderful, Alexa. It sounds like you have everything you ever wanted."

"And then some!" Alexa put a teasing note in her voice as Kurt came up behind her and wrapped her in a bear hug.

"Come on, gorgeous," he growled playfully in her ear. "I have plans for the rest of the day."

"Weddings always make him think of honeymoons," Alexa murmured to Sarah, then she squealed playfully as Kurt lifted her off her feet and nibbled at her ear.

"At least you always know that honeymoons make me think of you," Kurt stage-whispered to his wife, then added, "Hi, Sarah. 'Bye, Sarah. We'll be leaving now." He started for his car, playfully pulling Alexa along.

"I'll see you later," Alexa called over her shoulder as she followed her husband to their car. "Just remember what I said, Sarah. Nothing means anything until you have someone with you to share it."

"I'll remember," Sarah said, waving as the couple drove away. Under her breath she added wryly, "As if you'd let me forget."

She heard a footstep. "They're good together, aren't they?" Chris said, coming up behind her.

"Barely newlyweds themselves," Sarah answered, looking after their car. In that moment she envied their hopes and dreams, their unsullied faith in marriage, in each other. She didn't realize she had sighed until Chris responded.

"Is everything all right?" He stepped beside her, his hand at her back.

"Yes, fine," she answered brightly. "I guess weddings just make me . . . thoughtful."

"Me, too," he said, smiling, but the words seemed to carry more than the obvious meaning. "Look, do you have a few minutes? Or do you need to get back to something?"

She looked into Chris's open gaze and saw there a friend, someone she could trust. Her uneasiness ebbed, and she relaxed for the first time in weeks. "I have some time," she answered. "What do you have in mind?"

"I'd like your opinion about something," he said, guiding her toward the house. "Now that Mom has moved in with your dad, I have the old place to myself. I've been saving my money for years. I thought I might one day build a place of my own, but now I'm thinking about some remodeling projects here. I'd like to see what you think of them."

"You know that decorating and design aren't exactly my strong suits," Sarah demurred as they climbed the steps.

"If I wanted a *professional* opinion, I'd hire one," Chris teased.

She quipped back, "Okay, but you get what you pay for," and he laughed as he opened the door.

They made a project of it, touring from room to room, laughing often and enjoying each other's company. Chris showed her how he wanted to expand the dining room by adding a large bay window over the side yard, and Sarah could see how the simple change would open up the room, making it airy and light. He showed her where he wanted to take out the wall between the parlor and the dining room, creating a great room that would stretch across the front of the house. Sarah could picture it filled with McAllisters, a picture that tugged warmly at her heart.

Next he took her into the kitchen, where he showed her the remodeling his mother had done about three or four years ago, right after Jim and Meg got married, and how he wanted to extend the same plan onto the mud porch and pantry beyond. The plan made perfect sense to Sarah, who could see how much easier it would be to work from one room to the other when the house was finished as Chris planned.

He cracked the door into what appeared to be a large bedroom, then seemed to change his mind and closed it again. "Come on upstairs," he said instead, then took her hand, charging the staircase as if storming a castle.

"I'm coming, I'm coming!" she answered, amused and pleased by his enthusiasm.

He showed her his plans for remodeling the tired old bathroom upstairs, replacing the tiny bathtub with a grand new one, "maybe even a jacuzzi," and opening the sidewall into what was now empty storage space, putting in a large, comfortable shower stall instead.

"The finishing touch will be a solar window to replace this little guy," he said, tapping the old, sash-drawn window that had been there through his childhood. "I'd like the kind that sticks out a couple of feet from the outside wall and has shelves for growing plants."

"That would be perfect here," Sarah agreed, pulled along by his eagerness. The view of the backyard with its spreading oak tree, one limb graced by a kids' tire swing, would add joy to mornings in this room.

Next they went to the three upstairs bedrooms, the ones Joan and Jim had claimed, then the larger one Chris had shared with Kurt until Joan left home to be married. "I can't think of much to do with these except fresh paint and wallpaper," he said, "and maybe a couple of window boxes outside."

"You know what would be nice in this one?" Sarah asked, beginning to catch his vision as she looked at the larger room.

"Tell me," he answered, smiling his pleasure at the way she was joining in.

"Some built-in shelves," she said, "right along that wall and around the door. It would be a great place for toys and books, for a little boy or girl to keep . . ." She stopped, aware of what she had just said, what she had just been thinking. "It would be good," she finished lamely, her enthusiasm gone.

"You're right," Chris said. "It would." The small crease between his brows told her he had noticed her change in mood. He hesitated, then set his jaw and put a new smile on his face. "Well, that's enough touring for today. Do you have plans for dinner or shall we go find a hamburger someplace?"

Sarah put on a bright smile, trying to recapture the

mood she had just slaughtered. "I'd kill for a hamburger," she growled in exaggerated tones.

"Ah, the carnivore emerges. I doubt if killing will be necessary," Chris rejoindered, "but I'll keep it in mind if we can't find something soon." He took her hand and they bounced down the stairs together, laughing and carefree as children.

"I don't know, Eden. I'm so confused I can hardly think." Sarah munched at a carrot and cradled the phone against her shoulder.

"What's to think? The question is simple. You're attracted to your cowboy, you like him, but Sarah . . ." Eden paused meaningfully. "Are you in love with him? If you are, you need to rethink some priorities. If you aren't, it doesn't matter."

"Ugh." Sarah blew out a sigh. "You do ask the tough questions, don't you?"

"I'm your friend. It's my job."

Sarah could almost see Eden's pleased-with-herself expression. "Smug this morning, aren't you?"

"Yes, I am. And you, dear lady, are ignoring the question. Are you in love with Chris?"

Sarah drummed her fingers. "I don't know. I haven't dared think about it."

"Does it occur to you that you're going to have to think about it? Soon?"

Another sigh. "I don't know. I guess I've been hoping that if I didn't think about it, the question would go away."

"Is Chris showing any signs of going away?"

Sarah thought about the wedding yesterday, the intensity in Chris's gaze as he had followed her with his eyes, the impromptu tour of his home and the light tone between them as they'd shared hamburgers and french fries later, the fervor in his embrace when he had kissed her good night at her door. She sighed again. "No, he isn't going away."

"Girl, one of these days that handsome hunk of yours is going to pop the question. I suggest you start thinking about an answer."

"Maybe that's where my real problem is," Sarah said thoughtfully.

"Translation?"

"Maybe I already know I'm in love with him—"

"About darn time!"

Sarah grimaced. "I only said *maybe,* remember— and maybe that's the problem."

"Okay, back up the paddy wagon. You've found a gorgeous man who adores you and treats you like a queen, puts up with the moods that even I, your dearest friend, find hard to tolerate—"

"Oh, you saintly soul."

"—and respects your work to boot. You think you're in love with him. And somehow that's a problem?"

"He *is* wonderful, Eden, and whether I'm really in love with him or not, I know I care about him. I care a lot. Too much to want to saddle him with the kind of baggage I'd bring to a second marriage."

"You told me he knows all about Jake—"

"Not *all* about it. Not everything."

"You mean you still haven't told him about—"

"No. I haven't. Eden, I can't."

"I'd say it's about time for that, too." Eden took a deep breath. "Listen, Sarah. If he cares about you, if you care about him, he deserves to know it all. Maybe it won't even matter."

"But it *will* matter, Eden. You should have seen him yesterday, after the wedding. He was showing me all the renovations he plans to make to the downstairs, to the kitchen and front rooms and even upstairs, in the kids' rooms . . ."

"Okay, Eden. It's time. Just sit down with the man and say, 'Listen, Gorgeous. We need to talk.' "

"You make it sound so simple."

"And you're making it much too difficult—as usual. Time to move forward, Sarah."

Sarah's voice grew sarcastic. "Oh, right. Forward. Just like you."

Eden adopted a patient tone. "We can straighten out my life later. You are the subject of interest today. Look, Sarah. This might be your chance, and who can tell whether chances like this might ever come again? I say go for it. Just call me early so I can stand up with you at your wedding."

"Yeah, right," Sarah responded without enthusiasm, but she had to admit Eden had given her plenty to think about. And she did think about it, all through the next day while she vaccinated dairy cattle and treated saddle horses for worms.

Chris called that evening to ask if she'd have dinner with him at his home the next night, and she told him she'd love to. When she hung up, she promised herself she'd follow Eden's advice. She'd come home early tomorrow and dress up for their dinner—maybe wear the yellow dress she'd worn at the wedding. Then when they'd eaten and were feeling sated and comfortable, she'd say, "Listen, Gorgeous. We need to talk," or something like that, anyway. That decided, she went to find and press her yellow dress.

"It was delicious, Chris." Sarah put down her fork and scooted away from the table. "Did you do all the cooking yourself?"

"Um-hm. Mom taught us all when we were young."

"And not a shred of meat in it anywhere." She gave him a teasing look. "However did you manage?"

"Honestly?"

She nodded.

"I went to the library and got a book of recipes for a vegetarian diet."

She smiled. "Chris, you're amazing. Have you ever made tabouli before?"

"Nope, first time."

"It was wonderful. You're a quick learner."

"I try."

The moment stretched.

"Look, Chris—"

"Listen, Sarah—"

They both laughed nervously.

Chris stood and pushed his chair in, then pulled her

chair out for her and gave her his hand. "When I showed you my plans for the house, there was one place we skipped. I'd like to show it to you now, if you're game."

"Okay, then when we have a chance, there's something I'd like to talk about, too."

"Okay. Tour first?"

She stood, smiling nervously. "Sure."

Chris took a deep breath. He'd made up his mind when he kissed Sarah good night on the evening of their parents' wedding. It had taken a couple of days to get everything ready. Now he wondered if he had the nerve to carry it through.

"So where are we going?" she asked.

"I'd like to show you what I have planned for the master bedroom," he answered, taking her hand and leading the way. "It's a big room, right next to the office."

"I remember," Sarah said, remembering too the way he had closed the door on that room during the earlier tour.

They reached the door and this time he swung it wide, then motioned her through ahead of him. "It's a bit shabby right now," he said, "but some new paint and wallpaper will help . . ."

Sarah entered the room and looked around her. She could see the shabbiness, but she loved the room instantly. It had the same high ceiling and cornices as the rest of the house, and a wide, sash-drawn window with a view of the backyard oaks. Chris's small double bed sat against one wall, with a tidy dresser beside it, but there was plenty of space for more and larger furniture. She could picture a huge king-size bed, a pair of matching dressers, a lounge chair— She cut the images off, afraid to picture any more. "It's a lovely room, Chris," she said with genuine feeling.

He stepped close and put one arm around her. With the other he began to point out features he'd like to change. "I'm planning to install a ceiling fan," he told her, enouraged by her approval, "the kind with multiple light fixtures and two dimmer switches on the wall, one to control the light intensity, the other for fan speed."

"That will be nice."

"And here, where the window is . . ." He led her toward it and pulled back the curtain. "I want to put in French doors instead."

"You want to open the room into the backyard?" she asked, uncertain whether she had understood him.

"Onto a deck," he said, then took a deep breath for added courage. "I thought it would be nice to open this room out onto a patio built at the same level as the house." He opened the window wide and looked out. She felt his anticipation—whether eagerness or anxiety, she couldn't say—and her own heart rate raced to keep time. "I've already installed the outdoor lighting," he added. He reached beneath the curtain beside them and flicked a switch.

Sarah could feel him holding his breath as she leaned to look out the window. On the lawn outside the window, dozens of potted yellow tulips were arranged to spell the words, *I LOVE YOU, SARAh.*

Don't Promise Me Rainbows 129

"It was too late in the season for daffodils," he said, his voice shaking. "I found a hothouse in Phoenix that still had yellow tulips and I had them ship up all there were. I'm afraid there weren't enough to capitalize the 'h.' "

He was trembling. Sarah could feel it in his hand as he took hers. Tears had welled up in her eyes the moment she saw the flowers. Now she blinked to see through them as Chris knelt beside her and dropped to one knee. A tremor of alarm ran through her, and she suddenly wished Eden could be here to advise her.

"I've been thinking a lot about us, Sarah," Chris began, caressing her fingers. "I'm so in love with you, it hurts." He reached into his pocket and brought out a jewelry box, then opened it and held it out to her. "Sarah, my love, will you marry me?"

Sarah's hand shook as she took the box and looked at the ring—a huge, brilliant-cut diamond flanked by sparkling amethysts. "Oh, Chris . . ." she said, then swallowed, unable to speak.

He swallowed, too, attempting a smile. "Is that a yes or a no?"

She drew a deep breath. "I . . . I'm not sure."

He hesitated before pasting on another brave smile. "You know, this isn't quite the way I imagined this going."

She laughed nervously. "I don't suppose so." She licked her lips. "Listen, Chris. Can we talk?"

He took another long, deep breath, then stood. "Sure," he said, and braced himself for the worst as he led the way into the living room.

Chapter Eight

Chris entered Kate's parlor and turned on a lamp in the corner. "Have a seat," he offered, indicating a space on the sofa. "I'll stoke the fire." He forced a weak smile. "I'm expecting a cold front."

"Chris—" Sarah began, but the words in her mind were inadequate to comfort either of them. She stopped them and poised herself, legs crossed, hands primly on her knee, waiting for him to return.

He took his time with the fire, then came back to her, but instead of sitting beside her, he pulled up an ottoman and sat at her feet, then tenderly took her hand. His eyes were sad as he said, "Talk to me, Sarah. Tell me what's wrong."

Sarah saw how he straightened his shoulders. She understood his fear, and her heart went out to him.

Then she steeled herself to tell him the truth. "Some time ago," she began, her voice shaking, "we talked, and I told you about Jake and me." She paused, uncertain how to go on.

"I remember," he prompted.

She licked her lips, gathering her thoughts. "I told you there was more, that there were things about me you still didn't know."

"I remember that, too. I thought we'd taken care of that when you told me the rest, I mean, about the time he—"

"I know," she interrupted. "But that was only part of it." She folded her hands in her lap. "Chris, do you remember how I told you that I was eager to see Jake come home that last weekend? That I wanted to talk to him about something?"

He leaned back, "I remember."

"We never did have that talk," she went on. "He never knew that—" She dropped her eyes, then looked up, starting again. "On that last day, when we argued and he left, I was locked in the bathroom when he stormed out—"

"You told me that, Sarah."

"But I didn't tell you why I was so slow in following him. I couldn't pull myself together quickly enough because I was ill."

"Ill?" The concern in his face touched her. Even now, his thoughts were for her well-being.

"Morning sickness," she said, her voice barely above a whisper.

"Morning sick—" he repeated. Sarah watched as

the shock registered on his face. "You were pregnant?"

She nodded. "About five weeks. I was pretty sure before that, when we had that awful fight, but by the time he came home that last weekend, I'd seen a doctor and had it all confirmed."

He swallowed hard. "You had a baby?"

"I lost a baby," she clarified, "at about six and a half months."

His face registered the second shock. "I'm sorry, honey. That must have been awful for you."

"It was difficult," she admitted. "Jake hadn't been much of a husband, but he had unwittingly given me the best thing anyone had ever..." Her words stopped with a tremble, and a tear edged down her cheek. She wiped at it, then reassured Chris with a shaky smile. "When I was little, I used to wish I could have a family like other girls. Then when Jake wanted to marry me, it seemed like my chance. I wanted us to have a dozen kids."

She leaned forward. "By the time I got pregnant, I was pretty sure the marriage wasn't going to last, and I'd decided it would be better not to bring a baby into it—at least, not until we tried to work things out between us." She looked up again, taking courage from the concern in his eyes. "When I found out, I was delighted anyway. It didn't make sense, but I couldn't help myself. I couldn't stop thinking that even if I ended up divorced, I'd still have someone, I'd still have family."

"What happened?" he asked. "To the baby, I mean."

She shook her head. "No one ever knew. The doctor had theories. All we know for sure is, the baby died. I noticed it myself one morning. He'd been so active that I'd been teasing him about being a gymnast." She smiled and impatiently swiped at another tear. "One morning I noticed how quiet he'd become. Later that day, I began to feel the pains."

"You were in labor," Chris concluded.

She nodded. "The doctor said it was a normal reaction when a . . . a fetus died, that the body started labor in order to . . . shed it."

Chris sat beside her and hugged her close against him, trying to offer her comfort. "You called the baby 'he,' " he said after a time. "Was it a boy?"

"Yes. They let me hold him. I wanted to. He was so tiny and perfect." She paused again, her voice lost in memories. "The thing I remember most was his hair. He had a head full of it, thick and black."

"Black?" Chris, who had a hand full of Sarah's red curls, voiced his surprise.

"Like his father's," she explained. "The doctor said I didn't have to, but I filled out paperwork and arranged a burial, anyway. I named him Andy, Andrew Wiley McGill." She paused, her voice stopping on a sigh.

"Sarah?"

"Um-hm."

"Why did you feel you couldn't tell me sooner?"

"Because there's more, Chris." She stroked his

face with her hand. ''And it affects you, or at least, it will if I say yes to the question you just asked me in the other room, assuming you still want to ask it.''

''Sarah, you know nothing is going to change the way I feel—''

She put her finger to his lips. ''I know you say that now, but—''

This time he was the one who stilled her. ''Why don't you tell me whatever you have left to tell me?'' he asked. ''Then you can see that I mean what I say.''

''All right,'' she answered. She drew another long, deep breath. ''Andy's birth was difficult,'' she began again. ''It was complicated and messy, and nobody realized that anything was wrong until I began to get sick again a couple of days later. Dad thought I was just mourning my baby, so it took a while before we realized how bad things were getting. To make a long story shorter, it was bad. I had fevers and problems of all sorts and when it was over, I was pretty messed up inside. My doctor told me I'd be infertile, that I'd never be able to conceive again.'' She watched, waiting for the next shock to register. ''Do you understand what I'm saying, Chris? I can't have children. Not ever.''

Chris blinked once, then again. Slowly the realization crossed his features. ''Are they sure? You know, doctors can never be certain about things like that.''

She sighed. ''Oh, Chris. I know what you're feeling. Nobody wishes they were wrong more than I do, but the injuries to my body were extensive. The doctors said I would heal, and that there might be a slim chance I could conceive again one day, but they warned me not to count on it, and you can't count on it, either. If you still want me, you will have to give up the idea of having children, the same way I've had to give it up.''

"Oh," Chris said, but it came out more like a groan. She could see fresh realization dancing across his features and knew he was beginning to understand some of the unexplained events that had passed between them in recent months. "That's why you were always so hesitant around my nieces and nephew, and why you seemed so edgy around the baby."

"That's why I told Meg I didn't want to hold Alexis," she added, helping him understand.

"And why you got so sad in the upstairs bedroom the other day, when you were talking about the children who might live in that bedroom." He paused. "I'm sorry, sweetheart. I wouldn't have pushed any of that if I'd known."

"I know that, Chris, but at the moment this isn't about me."

"I don't understand."

"Don't you? You want what I wanted then, when I was younger—home and family, children of your own. You can still have that if you marry someone young and healthy, someone who can give you the family you deserve. I can't do that, Chris. I can never be that for you."

Chris swallowed a lump that might have been disappointment. "That doesn't matter," he said. "It doesn't, Sarah. It's you I want."

She looked at him sadly. "You can't deny you want a family."

"Of course I want a family, but we can adopt. Lots of couples do."

She sighed. "It isn't that easy. I know. I tried a couple of years ago as a single parent. There were tons of forms to fill out, all kinds of personal and sometimes embarrassing questions to answer, fees to pay up front, and no guarantee that anything would ever come of it. Even if an agency gave us a baby, there's no way to be sure we could keep it. You've heard the stories about birth mothers who come back after a year and a half, or two years. The courts always side with them, and the adoptive families end up losing the children they love." She shook her head. "It's not worth it. At least, not to me. I can't go through that, Chris."

She saw him digest that last information. He swallowed, licked his lips. "Look, Sarah, it doesn't matter. It's you I love, not the children we might or might not have together."

"You say that now, but you'd come to resent me in time, and I couldn't blame you for that." She pulled away from him.

"I wouldn't, Sarah," he said, his voice deep, but Sarah noticed that he made no attempt to stop her withdrawal.

"Don't promise me rainbows, Chris," she said sadly. "You don't know when the sun will shine."

He looked like he wanted to sob, and she thought of her childish responses when he had come too close to her before. She realized she had been thinking selfishly then, protecting herself at the expense of others. With an intensity so strong it nearly took her breath away, she knew now that she was really in love, enough in love to make the first truly unselfish gesture of her life. "Chris," she said, "you deserve so much more than I can give you. No one has ever treated me with the kind of warmth and generosity you've shown—"

"I love you, Sarah. I love you more than my own life."

She stroked his face, caressed his hands. "I love you too, Chris. More than I could ever have imagined. That's why I have to say no."

"No?"

She lifted her chin. "No. I'm sorry, Chris. I can't marry you."

Chris slammed a pair of hay hooks into a bale of alfalfa and wrangled it into place atop the twelve or thirteen bales he had already wrestled. He hadn't wanted to order hay, hadn't wanted to go on with any of the normal tasks of living, but whether he fed himself, or cared to, the beef calves still needed to be fed every day. He hooked another bale, then another, and another, until his muscles ached and sweat glistened on his bare upper body, but the work was doing nothing to relieve his anguish and frustration.

He smashed a hay hook into the wall, biting off an angry curse, but the splintering wood shattering around him offered no comfort at all. He cursed again and slumped against the stack, letting himself slide to the floor. Six days. It had been six days since he had proposed to Sarah, six days since she had turned him down, rejecting him for his own good. He snorted at the irony of it. In all the time since she had left that evening, she had refused to see him, refused even to return his calls. Once, two days ago, he had left in the middle of chores to be outside her apartment when she started morning calls. She had come as he expected, and they had talked, but only for a moment. Never meeting his eyes, she had told him to stop calling or trying to see her. "It's best this way," she had told him, then she drove away without answering when he asked, "Best for whom?"

He groaned, pulling his knees up and dropping his head into his hands. Part of him wanted to charge in, find Sarah, and make her listen when he promised it didn't matter; another part wondered if it did. He'd never been eager to settle down, but he'd always imagined that when he did, children would be part of that picture. Even on the day of the wedding, when he had first realized Sarah was the one, he'd pictured the two of them together, surrounded by little ones. When she'd told him there'd be no little ones, a part of him—he preferred to think it was a small part—had mourned that loss. Life without children would be nothing like the world he had imagined for himself. But life without Sarah? He couldn't picture that at all.

Wearily he struggled to his feet. When the wall phone rang, he had to push himself to stagger to the wall. "Rainbow Rock Farms."

"Chris! How you doin', White Eyes?"

"Logan! Great to hear from ya, buddy."

"So how come you don't sound great?"

"No biggie," Chris lied. "Same old, same old. Say, are you ever gonna get that place in Greasewood ready to house my pigs?"

"I know, I know. You're embarrassed for me," Logan answered. "But you know us Navajos. We've always had trouble with the white man's calendar."

Chris chuckled. "Take your time, pal. Just remember, these sows of mine are getting bigger—and more expensive—every day."

"That's fair," Logan answered. "Maybe it will help you get back some of what you should have asked for them in the first place."

Chris gave that thought a second. "You mean you knew you were cheating me?"

"Of course. None of the other farmers I'd dealt with were willing to settle for that little. I fully expected you to haggle. When you didn't, I just assumed you were distracted by the *belagaana* vet with the pretty red hair."

Chris hissed through clenched teeth.

"So how are things between you and the lady?" Logan pressed.

"Not," Chris answered with a sigh. "There are no things between us, no things at all."

"Ah, trouble in paradise. Don't tell me you didn't try . . ."

"Oh, I tried all right. Logan, I asked her to marry me."

"You asked her to . . ." Logan whistled into the phone. "My friend, you have it bad."

"I don't have it at all. She said no."

Logan paused a long three counts before he answered, "I don't believe it. Chris McAllister, lady-killer extraordinaire, has finally met his match."

Chris's laugh was dry and humorless. "Well, I thought I had. Listen, there's nothing we can do about my shattered love life, but I would like to see you get your farm project up and running. What can we do about that?"

"As a matter of fact, that's why I called," Logan began. He went on to explain where the holdups had been and how everything was finally being resolved. "So we can be ready for your sows Thursday, if you think you can get them here. The others are all being trucked in on Wednesday afternoon. If you and the pretty *belagaana* could come in the next day, she can do the final inspection and sign our papers while she's here."

"That may present a problem," Chris answered, then explained that Sarah had quit the project as well. "She told me to tell you to get someone else," he said, "and she isn't taking any calls from me. I don't know what to say, man. I'm sorry."

"So am I." There was a pause while Logan collected his thoughts. "Look, do you think you could prevail on her to come out just once more? I expect we can find someone else in time, but we have to have a licensed vet here on Thursday. That's only three days, and I don't know anyone I can pull in that fast.

I'll call her myself, several times if I have to, but I think we'll get farther if you call.''

Chris snorted in derision, but Logan went on. ''Talk to her, pal. Play on her sense of duty. We'll be up the creek if she doesn't come through for us.''

''I'll see what I can do,'' Chris answered as he hung up the phone, but he had his doubts. Still, this would give him an excuse to call Sarah again, maybe even to see her. He left the barn smiling for the first time in days.

Sarah pushed into her apartment and dropped on a chair. It had been one of the toughest days in her veterinary practice, and all she wanted now was for it to be over. To a schedule full of routine calls, she had added three serious emergencies. Two of her patients had died—in her opinion, unnecessarily—and she was sick with regret and frustration. She noticed the flashing light on her answering machine and groaned. Office calls she took over her cellular phone, so the only messages on her machine were personal, and lately, virtually every one was from Chris.

''Oh, Chris, I can't face you today,'' she moaned. It was like the old joke: seven days without Chris Mc-Allister had made her week—or was it weak? She almost turned the machine off. Then, on the slight chance that there might be a call from Eden or her father, she punched the button. Sure enough, the voice she heard was the one she least, and most, wanted to hear.

''Sarah, it's Chris. Listen, I get the message. You

don't want me to call. You don't want to see me.
Okay, I understand. But Logan called this morning.
He's finally got the Greasewood project back on line.
Most of the sows are being delivered on Wednesday
afternoon and I'm taking mine out Thursday morning.
If they don't have a licensed vet to do the inspection,
the whole project could collapse.'' There was a pause
and Sarah heard him struggling to control his voice.
''Sarah, if you don't want to see me, I can understand
that, but don't leave Logan's people in a bind because
of me. Call me. Please.''

There was a buzz, then a call from Logan Redhorse
that repeated Chris's message. The third call was also
from Chris, asking her to please call when she came
in, then there was a fourth, this time from Eden. All
it said was, ''Sarah, call me.''

Sarah picked up the phone. When Eden answered,
she said, ''Hi. What's up?''

''Is he still calling?'' Eden asked without preamble.

Sarah sighed. ''Yeah. He's as persistent as you are.
Eden, when are you going to accept that I'm right
about this?''

''Never. You're wrong.''

''Eden, you don't understand—''

''No, I don't!'' Sarah was surprised to hear anger
in Eden's voice. ''He loves you, you love him, he
wants to marry you and spend the rest of his life making you happy, and you won't even take his calls?
Girl, I never thought I'd hear myself say this, but you
are an idiot, certified and gold-plated.''

Sarah sighed. ''You didn't see his face when I told

him we'd never have children. He was heartbroken. Really devastated.''

"Of course he was. It took you a while to get used to the idea, didn't it?"

"Well, yes, but—"

"No 'but' about it, girl. He deserves a little time to get used to the loss as well. And you didn't exactly make him feel better by telling him to get lost.''

"It isn't like that," Sarah said, but the words fell flat on her own ears.

"Yeah? How many times has he called today?"

She bit her lip. "Twice."

Eden's sigh was long and exaggerated. "Call him, Sarah. Give him a chance. Give yourself a chance.''

"I'm afraid I'll have to."

"Hm? What do you mean, 'have to'?"

Sarah told her about the Greasewood hog farm and how she felt obligated to follow through with Thursday's inspection. "It would be foolish of me to think I could stay in this little town without ever bumping into Chris again. I guess I might just as well get used to the idea that we'll still see each other from time to time.''

"That's right," Eden said, her tone brimming with exaggerated brightness. "You'll be there to see him get over you and start dating someone else. If you play your cards right, you might even be invited to the wedding.''

Sarah hoped Eden didn't hear her moan. "Eden, I can't handle that right now.''

"Maybe you'd better think about it, Sarah. It's the

life you're planning for yourself. If you keep up what you're doing now, you just might get it.'' Eden dropped the phone in its cradle and Sarah found herself listening to a busy signal.

"What a day this has been," she mumbled, closing her eyes in physical and emotional exhaustion. When she opened them again, the message machine was still blinking. She had thought Eden's message was the last, but apparently she had cut the recording off before it finished its routine. Wearily, she punched the button again.

"Dr. McGill?" a timid voice asked. "I hope I have the right number. I'm looking for the Sarah McGill who applied for veterinary work here at the racetrack. The vet we hired for the position has opted to leave us for another job. Before we advertise again, we'd like to know if you'd consider joining us. Please call in the morning. The number is—" Sarah grabbed a pen and paper and jotted it down.

Maybe she'd found her answer. Her father and Kate would be home by the end of the week, and her dad was well enough to resume his practice. If she took the job in Phoenix, it would mean giving up many things she loved, but it would also mean she wouldn't be here to carry out Eden's grim forecast for her life. Promising herself she'd return that call first thing in the morning, she called Logan and told him she'd be there on Thursday, then she took several deep breaths to fortify herself and dialed the McAllister home.

It was a relief when the machine answered. She left a brief, businesslike message telling Chris she'd be in

Greasewood on Thursday, then she collapsed on her couch and slept almost three hours before she finally woke up enough to crawl into bed.

By the time Thursday dawned, three more things had changed in Sarah's life: she had rescheduled her Thursday appointments so she could give the Greasewood project its due; she had accepted the job in Phoenix; she had let Chris talk her into riding "out to the rez" with him. She was uneasy about seeing him again, but his argument about saving gas and his plea that she might remember and value their friendship had finally won her over. She had spent the past couple of days preparing herself to see him again. What she was not prepared for was the rush of joy that swept over her when she saw him striding up to her door, gorgeous in jeans and a denim jacket, his face warm with anticipation, his golden hair swinging behind him.

"Hi," she said, opening the door.

"Hi yourself," he answered, holding it for her and blowing on his hands to warm them. "Anything I can carry for you?"

"No, thanks. I've got it."

He stepped back as she came out, locking the door behind her. She started to walk toward the truck, but before she could take two steps, Chris caught her arm and turned her toward him. "There's something I need to get out of the way," he said, then before Sarah could protest, he pulled her against him and held her close.

It was heaven, sheer heaven. Sarah wished for the embrace to spin out into eternity. Encumbered by her clipboard and veterinary bag, she was unable to hold him as he held her, but she couldn't miss the warmth of Chris's hard body, the sheltering tenderness of his arms, the burn of his breath where it touched her cheek and ear.

"There," he said, releasing her much too soon. "That's how I greet a friend." He gave her a wan smile.

She beamed back at him. "Thank you, Chris. That means a lot to me."

"No problem," he said, then led her to the truck and helped her in.

Though they were often at a loss for words as they made their way out of Rainbow Rock, the hug had broken the tension and Sarah found that by avoiding the subject of their relationship, they were able to talk fairly easily. As soon as she thought it, the idea made sense. She and Chris had always been able to talk easily. In a few short months, he knew her better than any person alive, anyone except Eden, and she had shared with him some of her most precious moments, and most tragic memories. Of all the things she'd be giving up when she left Rainbow Rock for good, the one she would miss most was Chris McAllister's friendship. Whatever else between them was destined to die, it seemed a pity that the friendship would have to die with it.

"Chris," she said, "there's something I need to tell you." Then in brief, choppy phrases, she blurted out the offer from the racetrack in Phoenix and her tentative acceptance. "I still have to talk to Dad," she said, "but I think he's ready to resume his practice. When I've cleared that, I'll be on my way."

Chris made an odd, choking sound. He kept his eyes straight ahead. "How long?" he forced out, his voice little more than a croak.

"No more than a couple of weeks, I'd guess." It was killing her to cause him this much pain. She comforted herself with the thought that it would be better for him in the long run, that someday, when he had a beautiful young wife and a bevy of children around him, he would thank her for leaving.

"A couple of weeks." His words were filled with pain. He clenched his teeth and she saw his knuckles turn white where he gripped the steering wheel. "Sarah, you don't have to do this."

"I think it's best," she whispered.

The sound he made in answer was little more than a growl. There was silence between them then. After a long while, Chris asked, "Mind if I turn on the radio?"

She understood his need to fill the void. "Please do," she said.

He clicked it on, but just as he did, a country crooner belted out, "I'm gonna love you forever." Chris cursed under his breath as he snapped the radio off. Another silence ensued, then Chris spoke, a sound so low and quiet, Sarah barely heard the words. "I am, you know. No matter where you go, no matter how far away. You're a part of me, Sarah."

"Chris, please—"

He turned to her with a look of breathtaking intensity. "No, don't cut me off. I need to say this and I think you need to hear it."

"But really—"

"Sarah!"

She quailed. She had never seen Chris angry—at least, not with her. "All right," she said. "I'll listen."

He took a deep breath. When he spoke again, his voice was calmer. "I know you think you're doing the right thing, but you're treating me like a kid with no mind of my own—"

"Chris, I'm not—"

"Let me finish!"

She quieted.

"I'm not a child, and forgive me for putting it just this way, but I'm not an eighteen-year-old buckle bunny, either."

She winced.

He put his hand on hers, trying to take the sting out of his words. "Don't transfer your thoughts and feelings to me, Sarah, and don't make up my mind for me. Let it be my choice whether or not I want you, and I do want you, Sarah—just as you are."

"But Chris, in time—"

"In time, we'll face the same kinds of problems that all married couples face—some we know about and some we haven't guessed yet, just like everybody else."

"But why face what you don't have to face?"

He gave her a warm, open look. "What difference

does it make? Lots of couples marry, expecting to have kids. They don't find out they can't until they've been trying for years. At least we'll have the advantage of knowing in advance—"

"Chris, it doesn't change anything—"

"And you're too quick to cut options short, too. For every couple that has to give a baby back to its birth mother, there are hundreds, thousands, of couples who adopt and raise children they love for the rest of their lives."

"I'm just trying to spare you the—"

"You're just wimping out, Sarah."

"What? How dare you say—"

"I'm saying it because it's true." He gave her a wry grin; there was a twinkle in it. "Just because I love you more than breath, that doesn't mean I'm blind to your faults."

She fought her temper down. "Chris, I'm not trying to wimp out, and I'm not trying to hurt you. I'm trying to save you greater hurt down the road. I'm trying—" She paused. The tears were brimming. "I'm trying to do the first truly unselfish thing I've ever done in my—"

"But is your interest really unselfish? Or are you trying to spare yourself pain?"

"Chris—"

"Just think about it, Sarah. That's all I'm asking. Just think about it. And believe me when I tell you that I'm capable of making my own choices, and I choose you." He touched her to emphasize his point. "I choose you, Sarah McGill. You told me that I can't

promise you rainbows, and you're right. I can't promise rainbows for any given day, but I can promise that
if we try, there'll be some rainbows, some days. Isn't
that all anyone can promise?''

He paused and when he looked up again, there were
tears in his eyes. ''It's like that song on the radio said.
I'm gonna love you forever, Sarah, and if you go
through with this crazy plan to drive away and save
me pain, you're going to break both our hearts for no
reason at all.''

''Chris—''

''Just think about it,'' he said, then he turned on the
radio again.

Chapter Nine

"Looks like you're all set here." Sarah signed the last of the forms and handed the inspection report to Logan. "Nice job, guys. Everything looks good."

"Thank you, Doc." Logan offered his hand and she happily took it, knowing how much more it meant coming from him. "You've done good work for the People these last months. I'm sorry we're losing you."

"Well . . ." She shrugged, but seemed unable to find words. "Me, too."

"If you ever decide to come home, the Navajo nation will always be happy to work with you."

"Thanks," she said again.

"Ready?" Chris said behind her. It was the first time he had spoken to her since their conversation in the truck, hours before.

"Ready," she answered. She picked up her clipboard and medical bag and followed him toward the truck. He opened her door for her and helped her in, but did not speak as they started down the road.

Sarah turned and looked over her shoulder, saying a silent good-bye to the corrals and the barns, and the project she had helped to midwife and would not see grow to maturity. If she went through with her plans, this would be the first in a long series of good-byes—and one of the least painful.

As they drove along in silence, the truck bumping down the rutted road, Chris's tension seemed to fill the cab. Sarah knew he was thinking about their conversation that morning. She'd been unable to stop thinking about it all day long, and the thoughts had made her edgy. But something else was happening, and it made her even more nervous. Outside the shelter of their vehicle, storm clouds were forming in what had been clear skies this morning, and genuine thunder had begun to rumble in the distance. "That's peculiar," Sarah said, watching as two clouds bonded into one, shutting off their sunlight. "It was clear just a couple of hours ago."

"I think we may be in for snow," Chris said, his tone communicating a level of distress that seemed out of proportion to the situation.

"That's ridiculous!" Sarah answered. "It's mid May. People have been planting their gardens for days."

"Then they may well lose them," Chris said, picking up speed despite road conditions. "I'll try to get you back to town before it hits, but there's no way of knowing for sure—''

''It was warm this morning,'' Sarah argued, then for lack of a better argument, she repeated, ''It's mid May!''

''You've lived here most of your life,'' Chris said, his tone reasonable. ''Haven't you ever seen it snow this late? It snowed the night of my high school graduation, and that was two weeks later in the year than this.''

Sarah raised an eyebrow. ''Hmm, you're right about that. It snowed a little on the night I graduated, too.''

''And it's going to snow today,'' Chris predicted, casting a worried glance at the sky. Within half an hour, the weather proved him correct as lacy flakes drifted lazily from the sky.

''It's lovely,'' Sarah said as she watched the light flakes drift, beginning to powder their path. But the storm wasn't destined to be either lacy or lazy. Soon a blustery wind howled down off the sacred Black Mountain, driving heavier, wetter snow before it. Within an hour, the storm had reached such severe blizzard intensity, they could barely see beyond the nose of their own pickup and an inches-thick blanket of powdery white already obscured both the road and the landscape, making driving all the more hazardous.

''Are you sure we should be driving?'' Sarah asked as they plowed their way toward home. ''I honestly don't know how you can stay on the road.''

''We probably shouldn't be, but I don't dare stop,'' he answered. ''Who knows who or what might be coming along behind us? If we stop on the road out here, we'll be creamed by someone else who didn't stop and wasn't expecting to encounter roadblocks. If we try to pull off the road, given these conditions, we'll be lucky if our bodies are found before June.''

''Now that's a pleasant thought,'' she chided, but his eerie prediction was chilling her even more than the unexpected cold snap.

They continued creeping along as they turned onto the highway, Chris finding his way largely by guess-work and his limited view of the shape of the road, their speed often under twenty miles per hour. On a good day, a day like the one they'd had when they started this morning, they'd have been home before now. Instead they were still well inside the Dinehtah, the speed and chill of the storm intensifying by the moment. Within another twenty minutes, both ground conditions and visibility were so bad, Sarah became fearful. She started to speak, asking Chris for reassurance.

That's when they heard the engine. At first Sarah couldn't believe anyone else was out in this weather with them, let alone gaining speed.

''Sounds like another truck,'' Chris said, watching his rearview mirror for any sign of it.

''I'm surprised anyone else is out in this,'' Sarah began, but as she looked out the back window a red pickup truck came into view just behind them, then swerved to pass on Sarah's side, on the right.

''Look out, Chris!'' she called. ''He's passing on the right.''

"I see him," Chris answered, easing slightly to the left. Just then their wheels skidded wildly. Sarah screamed, grabbing for the door handle to brace herself against the force of the turn, and the inevitable crash.

"Sarah, hang on!" Chris shouted. The force of their spin flung the truck off the left side of the road and into new danger. Their truck was off the road now and axle deep in snow, still plowing along at highway speed. Chris fought to slow them down and to bring the truck back onto the roadbed, but the earth beneath them dropped away beside the road, falling rapidly lower the farther they went. When the roadbed beside them was almost even with their windows, their front tires dropped into a narrow ditch, then hit the steep bank on the opposite side, stopping them with a force that bounced the bed of the truck into the air and slammed them both forward into their seat belts before they settled with a hard thump.

"Are you all right?" Chris asked as soon as he recovered his breath.

Almost too terrified to think, Sarah forced herself to assess her true condition.

"Sarah, are you all r—"

"Yes," she answered, hoping to calm the distress she heard in his voice. "Yes, I think I'm fine. Do you . . ." Her voice quavered and she had to clear her throat to try again. "Do you know what happened back there?"

Chris popped his seat belt and slid next to her on the bench, then helped her out of her belt. He answered as he moved. "That other truck forced us onto the far side of the road," he said sensibly. "Then I think we hit black ice."

"Black ice," she repeated, rubbing at the bruises the seat belt had left.

Chris put an arm around her. "Sure you're okay?"

She took another breath. "Now I'm sure," she answered.

He put both arms around her. "I'm sorry I got you into this," he said, his voice tender. "I promise I'll get you home safely, but it may take time." He held her close and kissed her hair. "I'm glad you're okay."

"Chris?"

"Hmm?"

"How are we going to get out of this?"

He sighed. "I'm not sure yet. I need to look around a bit."

"No! Don't leave," she said, then heard the whine in her voice and said, "Sorry. I guess I'm still a little shaken."

"Me, too," he answered meaningfully, "but I need to check out our situation if we want to try to get out of it."

"Yeah, I can see that," Sarah answered. "But Chris?"

"Hmm?"

"Be careful."

"I guarantee it," he answered. He caressed her cheek, then opened his door. "Lock it behind me," he said.

She leaned on the button. "Locked."

He blew her a kiss and disappeared into the white-out. A violent shiver overtook her as he vanished, and she knew it was more from fear than cold. Sarah consciously willed herself to relax and begin the effort of reasoning herself out of her fear. After all, she was in charge of her own mind; she could control her own responses and use her own judgment. She could make her own decisions. The positive self-talk helped, and she felt more confident as she waited for Chris to return.

It seemed to take a very long time. Fearful images kept flitting through her mind of what might be happening to him out there, alone, in the cold. She dismissed each as soon as it appeared, but the lengthening time and the deepening cold both added to her anxiety, and she began to wonder what she would do if Chris did not return. Just when she was reaching the point when she felt she would have to do something, even if it meant going in search of him, he returned, knocking on the window first to assure her, then unlocking the door and quickly climbing in.

"Whew! It's cold out there!" He quickly shut and locked the door behind him, then dusted off the snow that remained on his clothes. "Has everything been okay here?" His look of concern touched her.

"Fine," she answered.

"Good." He blew on his hands to warm them.

"What did you find?" she asked.

"We're in pretty deep," he answered plainly. "I doubt we'll get the truck out without a winch. And

since we probably can't be seen from the road, well
. . . it looks like we may be here for a while.''

Sarah felt fear tightening her throat. Her voice was
small as she asked, ''What happened to the truck that
forced us off the road?''

''Hard to say,'' he answered. ''Looks like it just
went on.''

''Kind of him,'' Sarah said bitterly. ''Doesn't he
realize we're freezing out here?''

''Whoever it was probably didn't see us until he
was right on top of us,'' Chris answered calmly.
''Then once he'd gone by, he probably didn't realize
we were in trouble. The snow was so thick I doubt he
saw us go off the road. I'm sure he wouldn't have left
us if he knew we were in trouble. People out here are
pretty good at taking care of one another.''

''You're probably right,'' Sarah answered. ''But
Chris, what are we going to do?''

Chris blew on his hands again. ''I've been thinking
about that. I think we need to settle in for a while.''

''Here?'' Sarah shuddered. ''I sure wish I had my
cellular phone.''

''I wish you did, too, but since you don't, we need
to think about how to stay warm.''

''Stay alive, you mean.''

He folded his hands across himself. ''Same thing.
But I have an idea about that, too.''

''Can't we just turn on the engine and run the
heater?''

''We have roughly half a tank of gas, maybe a little

less. I figure we'd last a few hours, probably right into the coldest part of the night.''

She shivered again. Now it was more from the cold. ''Surely someone will find us before then.''

''How many someones have we seen since we came out here?''

''Good point.''

He cracked his door. ''I'll be right back. Same procedure as last time, okay?''

''Okay.'' She watched him go. ''Be careful!''

He nodded and disappeared into the storm again, but he reappeared within seconds. The strength of the blizzard was letting up and Sarah could see Chris now and then as he wandered near the vehicle, apparently picking up twigs and branches, bits of dry wood. He came back a few minutes later, holding one of the pickup's hubcaps, now filled with kindling. ''I think I left the morning paper behind the seat on your side,'' he said as he let himself in. ''Do you think you can find it?''

She dug behind the seat. ''Here it is.''

He put it on the floor beneath the steering wheel, then stacked several flat stones on top of it. Then, using a road flare he fished out from under the driver's side of the bench seat, he set the kindling afire. When it was burning well, he began adding larger branches to it. All the while, he kept the fire small, fully contained within the hubcap, with the newspaper and the stones serving as insulation, protecting the floor. When it was glowing, warming the cab, he said, ''Back in a minute,'' and left again, returning with a pile of small branches. He stacked them into the driver's seat and cracked open the window on that side. "Scoot into the middle," he said, "closer to the warmth. I'll let myself in on your side."

"All right," she said, and scooted. Chris fumbled in the tool kit in the back of the truck, then quickly joined her, easing open the window on the passenger's side door and a couple of the wall vents as well, "so we won't die of carbon monoxide or smoke inhalation in the night." Then he held up an Army-issue wool blanket, spread it over her, and climbed in beside her. He snuggled close and wrapped her in his arms. "I figure that between the warmth that little burner is offering, this wool blanket, and our shared body heat, we should be just fine."

"You carry a wool blanket with you?" she asked, feeling foolish since the evidence was already warming her sore shoulders.

"The high desert can be pretty unpredictable," he answered. "It's wise to be prepared."

"Smart idea, Chris," she commended, but she knew that she, at least, would draw more than warmth from his closeness. There was peace and comfort in his embrace, and an assurance that Chris wouldn't allow anything bad to happen to either of them. That was enough to take both the fear and the chill out of the storm.

Sarah awoke in the darkness, surprised to realize she had slept. She stirred and knew that Chris slept, too, his arms still tightly about her. Had it not been for their hazardous circumstances, their intimacy in the warm cab might have been pleasant, even enjoyable. The blizzard had stopped before nightfall, and Chris's homemade brazier had kept away the night's chill. The skies had cleared as completely as if there had never been a storm, and a nearly full moon lit the high desert, sending sparkling reflections off the blanket of snow. The anxiety of the afternoon had passed quickly, then as the daylight waned, Chris had melted some fresh snow to give them water to drink. Before darkness set in, they had each taken a brief, cautious comfort break in the area near the truck. All in all, they were as comfortable as conditions would allow, and closer than Sarah had imagined they would ever be again.

She sighed and snuggled warmly against the man she loved. Despite her efforts to keep her mind focused elsewhere, she had been unable to avoid thinking of their conversation yesterday. "Just think about it," Chris had urged her, and she had been incapable of doing otherwise, especially now when they were so warm and close. It was easy to imagine herself accepting Chris's proposal and welcoming a life filled with this warmth and closeness. Would it be selfish of her to do so? Was Chris right that it was really selfishness, her own fear of risking future disappointment, that had kept her from accepting in the first place? Huddling against him in the glowing midnight, she knew that life with Chris sounded ever so much more full and rich than the life she was planning without him—a contrast as sharp and vivid as that between the warm cab of the pickup and the icy bluffs beyond.

She remembered her self-talk when she sat alone in the cab the day before. She was right. She was indeed in charge of her own mind; she could control her own responses and use her own judgment. She could make her own decisions. And she could change them, too, if her first decisions were wrong, or based on flawed logic. So was her logic flawed? Chris had accused her of treating him like a child, trying to make his decisions for him instead of letting him choose for himself. Had she in fact been guilty of underestimating Chris? Or undermining his maturity? When she had been thinking of her choices as honest and unselfish, had she been distancing again, using her concerns for Chris as an excuse to keep her own heart safe?

She sighed and turned against him and he stirred, tightening his arms around her. ''Time for more wood?'' he asked drowsily.

She checked the brazier. ''Maybe. Shall I add some?''

''No, babe. I'll do it,'' he answered, and started to unwind his long body from its sleeping position, stretching his legs.

''It's okay. I've got it,'' she said, putting a small branch on the fire and watching to make sure the fire stayed contained.

''Thanks,'' he murmured. He stretched, snuggled, and slept again. He looked so open, so dear. Sarah stroked his soft hair and a rush of tenderness welled in her heart. She loved this man, more than she had ever believed she could love, so much that she would willingly sacrifice her own happiness to see him happy. But what if she didn't have to make that sacrifice? What if the way to make him happiest was to give in to her own desires to be happy?

She sighed and snuggled closer. Now, in the dark of midnight, sitting in the cab of a pickup under potentially threatening circumstances—this was the wrong time and place for life-altering choices. Still, she promised herself that when this crisis had passed, she would talk with Chris again. Then, if he still wanted her, she would try to make the choice that would offer both of them their greatest chances for happiness.

With her heart at peace for the first time in weeks, she rested her head against Chris's broad chest and let the flicker of the firelight lull her into sleep.

When Chris stirred again, the moon had long since set and gray light along the eastern hills heralded the time of morning that the Hopis called White Dawn. According to their legend, the sun left his night hogan clad in gray fox furs to ward off the early morning chill. It was not until he began to climb the sky that he put the furs away, allowing the yellow dawn to rise.

Moving carefully to avoid disturbing Sarah, Chris checked the fire in the brazier and added one last branch. By the time this fire had time to burn out, he hoped they would no longer need his makeshift heater.

His left arm, the one on which Sarah now rested, was tingling, and he carefully moved it out from under her, drawing her head against his chest. He knew this night on the desert had been nothing more than a respite in their stormy relationship, but at this moment he felt grateful to whatever power had brought them together and given him these few hours of peace with Sarah in his arms. He wondered again what would happen to them both in the days and weeks to come.

He knew how determined she could be. It must have taken remarkable strength and stubbornness for a widow, barely twenty, to struggle through a lonely pregnancy and the loss of the baby she had longed for, then to work her way through college and veterinary school, arriving at the top of her chosen profession. Based on that evidence alone he felt certain that once Sarah McGill had committed to a course, she would not easily be dissuaded. Still, if she went through with her plan to go to Phoenix, she would surely break his heart in shards and take a piece away with her.

"I just don't know how to stop her," he murmured into the quiet of the cab.

His words disturbed Sarah and she stirred, spilling flame-red hair over his shoulder and down his chest. Her arms tightened around him, holding him closer as she slept, and tenderness welled within him, so rich and full it threatened to drown out every other sensation. No, he didn't know how to keep her from making the monumental choice, and mistake, she now planned, but he vowed as he sat holding her that he would try. When their present crisis had ended, he would talk with her again and try to show her how much he loved her. He knew now that, children or no children, it was Sarah he wanted. Somehow he would find a way to show her that.

He was still holding her, silently promising his undying devotion, when he heard the sound of an approaching engine. For a few tense moments, he waited, hoping the sound wasn't just his own wishful thinking. Then a truck pulled up on the road alongside them and Logan Redhorse leaned out.

"Looks like you had a little problem," he called cheerily.

Chris waved, then gently shook Sarah's shoulder. "Wake up, sweetheart," he murmured. "The cavalry's here."

Chapter Ten

"How'd you know we were in trouble?" Chris asked as Logan's friends winched his truck onto the road.

"Not that we aren't glad to see you," Sarah added, smiling broadly as she joined them. "Hi, Logan."

"Hi, Doc," Logan answered, returning her smile. To Chris he said, "Deductive logic, man. When we saw that storm blow up, I figured I'd better check on you, so around the time I expected you to get home, I started calling both your place and Sarah's. When the time got late and neither of you had answered, I was pretty sure things had gone bad. . . ." He paused. "Either that, or you and the pretty doc had eloped to Las Vegas." He winked.

Sarah gasped, then felt her face warm as her cheeks

flooded with color. Oddly, it was a rather pleasant sensation. She smiled at Logan, who chuckled and went on. "Knowin' you, White Eyes, I figured either was possible, but when I thought about the doc, I was pretty sure you were in trouble."

Sarah chuckled and Logan continued. "I'd have come sooner, but it took me till this morning to locate a truck with a winch and some guys who were willing to come with me. I trusted you'd be okay on your own until then." He surveyed the brazier arrangement Chris had created to keep them warm, now dumped at the roadside. "Looks like I was right."

"Absolutely," Sarah answered, hugging Chris's arm. "Chris kept us warm and comfortable all night."

"I'll bet he did," Logan said, giving Sarah's tousled hair a speculative once-over.

"Tell me, buddy," Chris said, clapping Logan on the shoulder. "How'd you know we'd need a winch?"

"Didn't," Logan answered with a grin. "I have a five-gallon can of gas in the back of the truck, three spare truck tires, a generator and jumper cables, and a ten-gallon water bucket."

Chris shook his head in amazement. "Too bad you weren't a Boy Scout."

"I was, one of the originals. We Navajos were scouting before you white guys ever thought of it." He looked at the path their truck had taken when it slid off the road. "How'd this happen, anyway?"

"Another pickup came up on the right," Chris answered. "He forced us onto the other side of the road, then we hit black ice and that threw us off."

"Lucky you're all right," Logan said. He reached into his jeans pocket and brought out his keys, then sat idly fiddling with them. "Well, looks like we've got your wheels on the road again," he said. "Want to give the ignition a try?"

"Sure." Chris tried the key and it started immediately. "Looks like you've done it, buddy. Thanks so much for everything." He left the engine running while he spoke in Navajo to Logan's two friends, trying to offer them cash. They quickly refused and got back into their truck.

Logan walked closer. "Listen, White Eyes. If it's okay with you, I'd like to hitch a ride into Holbrook. My truck's at Sherwood's Garage getting a tune-up." He grinned at Chris. "So can I catch a ride into town?"

Chris looked quickly at Sarah. The time it took him to get her home might be their only chance to talk, and if he blew that, he wasn't sure she would ever give him another opportunity. Still, he owed Logan so much . . . Sarah smiled at him, a smile that looked like love and support. "Sure, buddy," he told Logan. "Hop in."

Logan spoke quickly to the men in the truck and they started their engine. He shut the door and clapped his hand against it in a parting gesture. As the men drove away he turned and strode back toward Chris. The three of them loaded into the cab of the truck— Chris driving, Sarah in the middle, Logan on the outside—and started down the road for Rainbow Rock.

Within ten miles they had driven out of the snow and onto dry roadbed.

"This is strange," Sarah said. "Are these storms often localized like this?"

"You never know about the weather out here," Logan answered. "But it is strange. Almost as if it happened just for you two." He gave Sarah an enigmatic smile.

Minutes later, he and Chris began sharing ideas about the future of the Greasewood project and gossiping about people they both knew. The break gave Sarah an opportunity to try to sort through her feelings about what Logan had just said, and about the myriad odd experiences of the past twenty-four hours. She thought of her sadness at leaving Greasewood behind, of her fear during the sudden thunderstorm so localized it seemed to have happened just for them.

Perhaps it did. The thought wrung a sharp gasp out of her, and both men paused in their conversation to look her way. She smiled reassurance and they resumed their conversation. Embarrassed, Sarah took a deep breath and looked gratefully at Chris. That storm could have meant disaster, even death, for both of them, but it hadn't, and the reason it hadn't was Chris McAllister. Through it all he had been the one constant, the solid foundation she could rely upon. Wasn't it possible that providence had smiled on them by giving them a reason to be together, and giving her a reason to trust? *Oh, Chris,* she thought, the words so clear in her mind she could almost hear them. *If you still want me, I'm yours.* He paused in his chatting and looked at her, almost as if he had heard her thoughts, then smiled a warm response. She could hardly wait for them to be alone.

They were about twenty minutes into their drive when Logan said, ''You know, I had a really interesting case come up last week.'' Chris raised an eyebrow, but since there was no other response, Logan went on. ''Seems the Navajo nation had a little problem they wanted me to handle at the medical clinic in Indian Wells.''

''What kind of problem?'' Chris asked.

''Early last week a girl walked into the clinic. The doctors guessed she was about eighteen and well along in labor. The staff explained they never handle maternity cases, but the girl delivered in the hallway while they were talking, then immediately asked for papers to give the kid up for adoption. She filled out everything as soon as they brought it, though it seems she used a false name, then she just disappeared. They assume she hitchhiked out of there.''

''What was she doing in Indian Wells?'' Sarah asked.

''She said a Navajo man was the baby's father,'' Logan answered. ''She told the people at the clinic that she wanted the baby to grow up 'with its own people' ''

''She isn't Navajo herself?'' Chris asked.

''Doctors weren't sure,'' Logan answered. ''She said she was, but they couldn't track her registration number. That's how they knew she'd used a false name.''

"She probably just wanted to get her medical services free," Chris offered wryly.

"Maybe," Logan agreed, "but the doctor figures the baby really is Navajo. Says he looks like an Indian kid."

The last phrase reminded Sarah of what Chris had said about Logan's *belagaana* grandparents, and she shivered, wondering how he felt.

"Did they look up the baby's father?" Chris asked.

"Couldn't," Logan answered. "The girl said she didn't know his name."

"That's too bad," Sarah said, her voice low. There was a heavy undertone in Logan's voice. He obviously meant for them, or maybe just for her, to derive some special meaning from his story. She suspected she knew what it was.

"So what do they want you to do?" Chris asked.

"Seems somebody had to figure out what to do with the kid," Logan responded, "and because I'm on retainer, I got stuck with the problem."

Sarah shivered, then shivered again—shudders that had nothing to do with the cool air in the pickup cab. She was reminded of Meg telling her the story of her courtship with Jim, of Alexa telling her about why she had married Kurt when she hadn't planned to marry at all. She realized Logan was telling his story for the same purpose, trying to help bring her together with Chris. She felt touched by his gesture, the warmth in her heart belying the gooseflesh on her arms.

"So what are you going to do?" Chris asked, playing the straight man for Logan's story.

"I did it yesterday morning before you two came out to the project farm," Logan answered. "I found the kid a family."

Chris and Sarah exchanged a quick look and Sarah turned toward Logan. "How did you do that?" she asked.

"We placed him with a Navajo couple on the rez. The nation is small enough without giving our babies away."

"That sounds good," Sarah answered quietly.

"You should have seen them," Logan continued. "The wife had cancer when she was in her teens and knew she'd never be able to conceive. The husband knew it too, long before they were married. They'd been registered with the tribal service for almost three years, and were afraid they'd never have kids at all." He paused, shaking his head with what looked suspiciously like sentiment. "You should have seen them," he said again. "They looked at that little kid like he was made of gold. The mother just kept running her fingers over the baby's head, saying what beautiful, soft black hair he had."

Like Andy's, Sarah thought. Her throat tightened. "It must have been wonderful for them," she said, her voice low. She was thinking of the mother who had gained a child and she nodded, remembering the joy as well as the anguish.

"It was," Logan answered. "I could see that. And you know what else I could see?"

Sarah couldn't stop herself from asking. "What?"

"I could see how good it was going to be for that little boy. That man and woman love each other. Even a tough nut like me can see it. They love each other and they're going to love that little baby. It was good to see them together. They're going to make a great family."

Logan paused, playing with his keys again. "Makes me feel good to know I've brought them together." He paused again, more meaningfully. "I noticed something else," he added, "something that made me smile. I noticed that they already were a family, even before that baby came to live with them. There was enough love in that little tarpaper shack to brighten up the whole place before that kid and I ever walked through the door."

There was silence in the pickup truck. "Yep," Logan said, repeating his point. "Babies or no babies, that husband and wife were already a family."

Sarah saw Chris's hands tighten on the steering wheel. She kept her eyes on her own hands as she fought with warring emotions. Logan didn't know it, but his speech was unnecessary. Sarah had already decided she would gladly marry Chris if he still wanted her. Still, it touched her that Logan, the Copper Crusader who disliked *belagaana* women, obviously cared this much about both of them.

The silence in the cab continued as Chris pulled the truck to a stop in front of Sherwood's garage. "Well, looks like we're here," Logan said, grinning as comfortably as if he hadn't just rocked their world. "Thanks for the ride, good buddy."

"Sure," Chris answered quietly. "Thank you, too." He reached across Sarah to shake Logan's hand. "It's a true friend who gets up early just to pull you out of a ditch."

"No problem," Logan answered. He turned to Sarah. "You take care, Doc. Give us a call whenever you're in town."

"Thanks, Logan. 'Bye."

"*Yah-ta-hey.*" He nodded in respectful acknowledgment, then walked into the garage.

Chris put the truck in gear, then looked at Sarah. "How come he gets to call you Doc?" he asked.

She smiled. "I like Logan."

"Ouch. Wounded to the heart." Chris put his hand over his chest and adopted a woeful expression. He pulled the truck into traffic, then his tone grew more serious. "Listen, Sarah, do you mind if I don't take you home just yet? There are a couple of things I'd like to talk about."

Sarah nodded. "I think we need to talk," she agreed. "But let's go to my place, anyway. We can talk there."

"Sounds good," Chris responded, and turned the truck in that direction.

The silence lengthened between them as they drove across town, parked in front of Sarah's apartment, and went inside. She needed to think of something to reduce her tension. "If you don't mind, I'll take a minute to freshen up,'' she said as Chris closed the apartment door.

"Go ahead,'' he answered. "Take your time. Have a shower if you like.'' He looked around the kitchen. "Okay if I start some hot coffee?''

"I'd love that,'' she answered as she disappeared into the bedroom.

Sarah hurried through a quick but thorough shower, wound her hair into a braid, put on clean jeans and a T-shirt, then snuggled into a thick, wool sweater and warm socks. She went back into the kitchen dining area to find Chris setting out a complete breakfast for two: scrambled eggs, toast and jam, coffee, and some fresh fruit from her crisper. She sighed. "You've got to stop this, Chris,'' she said, obviously loving it. "You're spoiling me.''

"I'd love to spoil you,'' he answered, stepping close enough to touch her still-damp hair. A new kind of tension filled the room. He gave her outfit a quick once-over. "You look . . .'' He paused, shaking his head. "Under the present circumstances, it's probably better if I don't say what I'm thinking.'' He tossed her a devilish wink and she felt her face warm in response. "Mind if I freshen up, too?''

"Not at all,'' she answered, recovering her voice. "There are fresh towels in the cupboard. Help yourself to whatever you need.''

"I'll be back shortly,'' Chris said as he traded places with her. "Go ahead and start breakfast if you like.''

"I'll wait,'' she answered.

Sarah sat at the table as Chris called from the bathroom. "You don't happen to have another sweater, do you?"

She chuckled. "Sorry. None that would fit you."

"Umm. Too bad." He disappeared behind the bathroom door. Moments later, Sarah heard him whistling as the shower went on.

She sat at her kitchen table, basking in the warmth of their shared intimacy. Sitting here acting very much like a wife waiting for her husband, she could easily picture what their life together would be like. Of course, she couldn't know whether she'd finally managed to persuade Chris that he really didn't want her, but the way he had looked at her just now gave her hope. She fidgeted with the fringe on her tablecloth while she waited for him to join her.

It didn't take long. Only minutes passed before Chris emerged, toweling his blond hair. He wore the same clothes he had worn since yesterday morning— the jeans tightly fitted, the shirt open. As he came out, he grinned at her, his cheeks dimpling. He looked positively delicious. She sighed and stopped her thoughts, wary of where such musings might lead.

"Still waiting?" he asked as he tossed the towel into her laundry hamper and finger-combed his hair.

"Um-hm."

"You didn't need to, you know."

"Seems only fair, since you were good enough to cook."

He sat beside her, taking her hand. "Would you mind if I offer grace?"

"Please," she answered, and bowed her head.

Chris's simple prayer touched her more than anything that had passed between them since their rescue that morning. He thanked God for their safety and good friends like Logan. He asked for a blessing on the food, then for wisdom and "clarity of thinking" while they talked. He asked that what was best for all concerned would come to pass, then humbly closed.

"Amen," Sarah responded, wanting more than anything for the two of them to be blessed with divine wisdom. She knew well what she wanted, what she had wanted all along. What she still didn't know was whether she was right to want it, and whether wanting Chris was fair to him. She picked up the bowl full of scrambled eggs. "May I dish up for you?"

"Help yourself," Chris answered. "I'll take what's left."

"You know," she said, "the tension is growing in here again."

He smiled wanly. "I know. I feel it, too."

"Maybe it would be better if I just said what I have to say."

He shook his head. "I think maybe I should start."

"Really, Chris, I—"

He took her hand. "Please, Sarah. There's something I have to say before I burst wide open."

The look on his face suggested he meant it. She retreated, setting the untouched eggs back on the table. "All right. You first."

He took both her hands and turned to face her so

their knees met. "Sarah, I can't let you go," he said. "I love you too much to give you up without a fight."

"But Chris—"

"It's like Logan was saying in the truck a while ago. Children or no children, we can be a family. And your telling me that you're turning me down for my own good is making me nuts. I mean, I'm a crazy man. I can't eat, I can't sleep, I forget things . . ." He paused, running his hand over his damp hair. "Two days ago, I put a pregnant sow in standing racks in the nursing pens and a new mother into farrowing. If I hadn't gone back later to find the piglets rooting around looking for their mom, I don't know what might have happened. And I can't imagine what I'll do if you pack up and leave me. I may have to ditch the farm and move to Phoenix."

"You can't do that, Chris."

"I can if it means I don't have to lose you." The intensity in his eyes certainly looked like he meant it. "I can do whatever I have to—"

"It wouldn't do any good, anyway." She squeezed his hands.

His face fell. "Are you that dead set against marrying me?" He looked like he wanted to burst into tears, or slam something inanimate into a wall.

Sarah almost chuckled, he looked so dear. "No, Chris. It's not that. It's just—"

"Don't tell me again that you love me too much to marry me. I may not be responsible for my behavior if you say that again."

"But I have no intention of saying that."

"But you just said—"

"I said it would do you no good to pack up and move to Phoenix."

He looked perplexed. "Okay. Why not?"

"Because I'm not going to be there."

"What? I mean . . ." He paused and rubbed his forehead. "I'm really confused here."

Sarah leaned forward, her face within inches of his. "Chris McAllister, you are the dearest, sweetest man I have ever known. I love you more than I had imagined it would be possible to love another person. I love you so much I was willing to give you up because I thought you'd be happier without me."

"But—"

"Shh," she said, tenderly laying a finger across his lips. "Let me talk for a minute."

He hesitated, apparently willing to let her speak.

"Last night, during that snowstorm, I would have died if not for you. Or at very least, I'd have been in big trouble. You were angry with me because of what I'd said earlier—"

"Not angry, really, just—"

"Shh," she repeated, louder this time. "You were angry, and I don't blame you. But in spite of that, you treated me with such love and care. Love is a feeling, Chris, but it's also a word, one people can use to get what they want, whether they mean it or not."

"It's not like that with me," he began, but she cut him off again.

"I know it's not," she answered. "Don't you know I know? I've been there, Chris. I know what that's like. The one thing most people don't realize about love is that it's more than either a feeling or a word. When you really mean it, it's an action.''

''An action?''

''A way of behaving, maybe. You don't have to tell me you love me, because you show me in everything you do—in the way you speak to me, in the respect you show me even when you're angry or hurt, in the way you look out for me first, making sure I'm taken care of before you take care of yourself.'' She covered both his hands with one of hers and lifted the other to touch his face. ''You don't have to tell me you love me, Chris, because you *love* me every day. Still, I hope you will keep saying it, every day for as long as we both live.''

She watched hope dawn in his expression. ''Are you saying—''

''I'm saying that if you still want me, I'd be honored to be your wife.''

''If I still want . . .'' Chris glanced heavenward. ''The angels know how much I want you, Sarah. You are the woman I've waited for, the only one I want. And we'll be a family together, you and me, kids or no kids.''

''That's what Logan said.'' She cocked a brow. ''I assume you told him about us?''

He looked shamefaced. ''Yeah, I did. I hope you don't mind too much, but I had to talk to somebody.''

''I understand,'' she answered. ''I told Eden.''

''You did? I'm curious. What did she say?''

"She said I should stop 'distancing' and marry you as soon as I could."

"Smart woman. I'm going to have to meet this Eden."

"I want you to," Sarah agreed. "Maybe at our wedding?"

"Sounds good to me. And how soon do you think we can arrange that, Mrs. McAllister?"

"Our parents managed it in a month, and their wedding was one of the loveliest I've seen. I would like invitations, though. Shall we say six weeks?"

He looked at her wall calendar. "Let's see. Six weeks from today is—"

"—the fourth of July," she finished with him, watching where he pointed. They both chuckled, then Sarah added, "It seems fitting to gain dependent status on Independence Day."

"For both of us," Chris agreed. "We'd never forget our anniversary." His eyes were twinkling, blue as the summer sky.

"And the fireworks seem appropriate, too," Sarah contributed.

"For us, they always have been." Chris leaned forward and kissed her as if to prove the point. He lingered there, tasting and enjoying the moment. "It's official, then?" he asked finally. "You're really going to marry me?"

"That's the plan," she said.

"And you're not going to change your mind? Or find some reason why I'd be better off without you?"

She shook her head. ''Not this time. You're stuck with me, cowboy.''

''And I couldn't be happier about it.'' He kissed her again to embellish the thought. Then, ''Let's go tell Logan,'' Chris said quickly. ''He had some errands in town. If we hurry, we'll catch him before he heads back to the rez.''

''Then Dad and your mom,'' Sarah added. ''Then I'll call Eden, then we can start in on the rest of your family.''

''And along the way, we'll stop off at my place and put that ring on your finger, just in case you forget.''

''I won't forget,'' she promised, her voice husky. ''Once I make up my mind about something, I am not easily dissuaded.''

Chris smiled wryly. ''I've noticed that about you.'' He picked up the bowl full of eggs. ''Do you want to eat breakfast before we leave?''

''Not unless you do,'' Sarah said. ''I'm too excited to eat.''

''Well, I'm starving.'' Chris shoveled eggs onto his plate. ''I think getting engaged makes me hungry. But I can eat while you're getting dressed. We'll leave as soon as you're ready.'' He dug in his fork.

''It's a deal.'' Sarah dropped another quick kiss on his mouth before he had time to fill it. ''But eat quickly. I won't be long.''

''Don't worry,'' he answered as she headed to her bedroom. ''I'll be here as long as it takes.''

''Now that's something I've noticed about you,'' Sarah said, giving him a playful pinch as she passed.

Soon they were back in Chris's truck, driving to share their news with everyone who loved them, with all those who had wished them to be together. "Look," Chris said as they turned a corner and faced the eastern storm clouds. Rain was falling along the hills and the sun shone toward it. "If we watch long enough, we might see a rainbow."

Sarah smiled, letting the warmth in her heart light her face. "It doesn't matter," she answered. "As long as you love me, I'll have everything I need."

"Then you'll never be needy again," Chris promised, squeezing her close beside him. "Or lonely, either."

They drove toward the hills, sharing each other's warmth. There were no rainbows, but the road ahead of them lay straight, the pathway smooth.